Stories from history

David Oakden

Illustrated by
Peter Kesteven
Tony Morris
Michael Whittlesea

Oxford University Press

Contents

Oxford University Press, Walton Street, Oxford, OX2 6DP
© David Oakden 1983
First published 1983   Reprinted 1986, 1988, 1990
Filmset by Oxford Publishing Services, Oxford   Printed in Hong Kong

Hoona's ring-stone   *Pre-Roman*

The village round-house was filled with evil-smelling
smoke and it was all Hoona's fault. Angry faces
grumbled and shouted at her through the gloom. Hoona
wiped a black smear across her tear-stained face and
again tried to explain to her mother what had happened.

'Mother, I did not mean to do it. It was all his fault.'
She pointed to a crawling baby boy, one of many
belonging to the families in the house. The naked child
was now sitting by the doorway playing with some
pebbles.

'He was playing near the big fire,' said Hoona. All I did was pick him up to move him away so that he would not get burned or trodden on.'

'You dropped him,' said Hoona's mother in her cross voice, returning to her task of grinding grains of corn into flour. It was heavy work turning the rough grindstone, and that was helping to make her cross.

'The baby wriggled,' said Hoona patiently. 'And I caught my foot against one of the fire-logs. It wasn't my fault that it was the one holding the cooking pots.'

'The men will be angry,' said her mother. 'Pots have been broken. Now clay will have to be dug and many new pots made. The men are busy at their work and will not want to stop to make pots. Also the food fell on the fire; it is spoilt and smells bad.'

The cloud of smoke made by the burning food was clearing slowly but it was true, the smell was bad.

'What are the men working at?' asked Hoona.

'Men's work,' said her mother wearily, stopping work to rest her tired shoulder. 'It's important, or so they say. Go and ask them.'

Hoona wasn't sorry to get away from all the anger, so she stepped over the baby and wandered out of the round-house.

A cool autumn breeze tugged at her clothes and she shivered a little. Soon it would be winter and then there would be mud and snow and dark nights. Already there were drops of cold rain in the wind.

Hoona picked her way through a herd of rough-coated pigs. She walked past two or three smaller, grass-thatched houses and down a rough track to where the men were working. Most of the men from the village seemed to be there and the girl watched them with curiosity for a while. She was puzzled by what she saw.

Some of them, as many men as she had fingers on both hands, were digging a trench into the chalky soil with rough pickaxes made from deer antlers. A second group, including Hoona's father, were using flat bones to shovel this soil into large wattle baskets. Yet another group of men and boys were dragging or carrying the full baskets away and tipping the soil on to a large mound. A circular rim of stacked turf stopped the soil falling back again into the ditch.

Hoona strained her eyes against the wind-driven rain but could not make out what the men were doing.

'Why are you doing that, father?' she asked. Her father paused in his work and looked up at her. But instead of answering her he just pointed at the mound. An older man working next to him scowled and told her to go away.

'This is man's work, girl,' he said snappily. 'Go where you belong with the women and stay out of our way.' He was big and fat and when he spoke his face wrinkled with anger.

Hoona shrugged and turned to go away, but as she did so she slipped on some loose stones and fell sideways against the fat man. She put out her hand to save herself but unfortunately it hit him on the chest and pushed him sprawling into the wet ditch. He yelled and spluttered as a shower of soil and pebbles came after him.

Hoona ran for safety, followed by the shouts of the man. She ran out of the cluster of huts, across the short grass where the chief's sheep were grazing, over the edge of a humpy earthwork, down into a grassy ditch and out again, and so into the circle of high ground where the big stones stood.

As she came to the first stone she stopped. By now the shouts of the man had died away. Looking back she could see that they had all gone back to work. She also noticed that smoke was no longer coming out of the doorway of the round-house. Now that she was out of the village things seemed to have got back to normal. She sighed. It had not been a good day.

Hoona looked up at the huge stone which towered above her into the cloud-dark sky. Then she walked all round the vast circle of stones, most of them far taller than any man, and all standing upright on their ends.

Having gone all the way round the circle and come back to her starting place, Hoona walked into the centre of the ring of stones. Here there were stones, even larger than the others, but this time lying flat on their backs, just like two giants having a sleep. She sat on the edge of one of them to rest. She often came here when she was in trouble, and seemed to find some comfort just from touching the stones. They were all so still, and so huge, and so full of mystery and magic.

Once she had asked her father about why the stones were there and how they had got there. But he had given strange answers, answers that she could not understand, answers that seemed to make no sense to a little girl.

It had all happened so long ago, her father had said, that no man alive now, nor their fathers, nor their grandfathers, could remember a time when the stones were not there. But the story was that many men from many villages had dragged the stones there from a place two days' walk away. They had dragged them to this spot, where the earthwork and the ditch already were, and had set them up on end. Clever men, men like their prayer-man, had worked with them, using sticks to help space the stones.

Again Hoona asked him for a reason, but her father had just shrugged his shoulders and said, 'Man's work, just man's work,' as if that were explanation enough.

Later on he had taken her out on a cold, frosty night when stars burned white in the winter sky. They had climbed over the ditch and stood by one of the large stones, waiting. Nothing happened for a time, and then, over the edge of the hills crept the full moon, its white light throwing harsh shadows across the circle where they stood. One of the larger stones threw a very long shadow, directly across the circle and almost touching their stone, the one they were standing by.

'See,' her father had whispered. 'Tomorrow the shadow will fall exactly on this stone, and that will be the sign that winter is turning, that longer days and warmer weather are on the way.'

Hoona still had not understood, and she had not been allowed to go with the men the next night when they went to the circle to make chants and to ask the gods to send warm sunshine.

Hoona sat down now on one of the two large flat stones, and ran her fingers round the strange design carved into it. This design was shaped like three or four small rings, each one inside the next. A straight carved channel came from the central ring and ran through the others to the outside like a rat's tail.

Hoona had also asked questions about these marks, but again nobody had seemed to want to tell her why they were there or what they were for. Perhaps nobody knew — certainly they had been there for a very long time. 'It is man's work,' said the grown-ups again and again.

Suddenly Hoona had a thought and ran off to one of the tall stones. Down near its base the soil was soft and Hoona scrabbled in it for something she had hidden there some time before.

It was a small, round flint, about the size of a water-fowl's egg but it had a smooth hole going right through the middle of it so that the whole thing looked like a clumsy ring. She slipped her middle finger through the hole and clutched it in the palm of her hand. At once she felt somehow comforted and safe, and she sat down with her back to the large stone.

How long she sat there Hoona did not know. Perhaps she slept for a while. When she opened her eyes again it was to see a small group of men from the village just walking into the circle. One of them was their chief, another was the old man who led the prayer-chants to the gods. The others were carrying a dead sheep. Hoona got up and crossed over to them.

'What are you doing?' she asked.

'Go away, girl,' said the prayer-man with a scowl. He had never had a kind word for her in the whole of her life. 'Go away. This is man's work.'

'But I want to watch,' she said.

He scowled again, but obviously couldn't be bothered to argue. 'Well, watch then, but keep quiet, and do not interfere.'

The men had started to dig a hole in the ground using deer-antler picks, just at the edge of the circle.

As they continued the prayer-man suddenly started to wail in a high voice, making a chant to the gods. The others joined in, and Hoona strained her ears to try to catch some of the words.

From what she could hear the sheep had died of an illness, and the prayer-man was making a chant to ask the gods to spare the other sheep in the flock.

One of the men, using a bronze axe, hacked a leg off the dead animal and dropped it into the hole to bury it. Then he knelt down and placed the axe in the hole also, blade pointing upwards. Another man put in a shallow bowl with the other objects. Finally the soil was shovelled back and the whole place stamped down. More chants were sung, and then the men moved off carrying the rest of the sheep's body.

Hoona let them get out of sight and then ran over to where they had dug. She could not believe what she had seen. She could understand them burying part of the sheep, and she knew that the buried bowl was an offering to the gods. But nobody in their senses would bury anything as useful as a bronze axe, she thought.

Axes were very precious, and her father did not own one at all. He would certainly be very pleased with her if she could dig it up and take it to him. She began to dig with her fingers in the soil.

All of a sudden she felt a tremendous blow on the back of her head which sent her sprawling and howling. As she got up she saw that the prayer-man had crept back while she wasn't looking, and that it was he who had struck her. He was standing over her now, screeching with rage. Lifting his hand he struck her again in the face, making her lip jag against a tooth. She felt salt blood on her tongue and she howled with pain and fear.

The prayer-man yelled at her to leave things alone, and stamped the earth flat again. Then he walked away with a final curse and a threat.

Sobbing, and wiping the blood from her mouth,
Hoona ran to the nearest big stone and curled up against
it. She clutched at her little ring-stone for comfort and
rocked backwards and forwards with pain.

15

After a while she felt a little better. Noticing a drop of blood on the ring she put it to her mouth and licked it. Then, without thinking what she was doing, she lifted it to her eye and looked through it.

It was then that something very odd happened. As she looked through the smooth round hole it was as if she could see things that weren't really there.

Instead of the empty circle of stones in front of her she seemed to see a misty picture of the men burying the sheep, just as they had done. She saw again the axe and the bowl. The picture faded and then another took its place, this time of the prayer-man hitting her and then striding away from her.

Hoona was not frightened. It was something she could not understand, but there were many things like that. She stood up, putting her hand on the tall rock, and finding with her fingers another of the curious circular carvings. As she ran her fingers round the circle she found herself crooning a soft chant about how she hated the prayer-man and about how he had hurt her. She chanted about what she would do to him in return, and then she lifted the ring to her eye again.

The picture was quite clear this time. It was as if she were looking into the big round-house from the doorway. The prayer-man was there, lying crumpled on the ground. One of his legs was twisted awkwardly under him. Her mother was there looking anxiously at the leg.

Hoona came to her senses again with a start, and discovered that she had been clutching the ring-stone so tightly that it had marked her fingers. In spite of the cold of the day she was sweating.

Slowly she walked back to the village, feeling chilled and shivery. As she crossed the ditch and earthwork she could see the mound the men were making. It was going to be very big, as far round as the whole village itself, and with sloping sides. It would take the men many months to build. She wished someone would tell her what it was all about.

The men were not working any longer. As she approached the round-house she was surprised to see a small crowd of people round the doorway, peering inside. Something had happened, and she remembered what she had seen through the ring-stone. The hair on the back of her neck began to prickle.

Hoona wriggled her way through the crowd and got into the hut. It was just as she had foreseen. There on the floor lay the prayer-man, his leg bent awkwardly under him, with her mother looking at it anxiously. A baby was screaming in its mother's arms.

Hoona knew what had happened this time without asking. At the same time as she had been making her chant about the prayer-man he had been rushing into the round-house to tell her family what an evil child she was. He had probably tripped over the baby near the door and had fallen. Hoona knew that his leg was broken and that he would probably die.

Nobody said anything to the little girl in the shadows near the doorway. But suddenly the prayer-man looked up and met her eyes. Gradually Hoona realized that she had no fear of him, but that he had great fear of her. He knew that she had some strange power, greater than he had ever had. He closed his eyes as she began to smile.

As the people began to wail a soft, sad chant, Hoona clutched her ring-stone and sat back in the gathering gloom of the dying day. After a long time her smile faded and she slept.

Clement, master dreamer   *Roman*

Spring came early that year. On the trees around the
Roman garrison town of Galava the fruit blossom hung
pink and white in the gardens of the great villas.

In the narrow streets soldiers, free at last from their
winter clothes, rubbed shoulders with British families.
Shop doorways stood wide open and from the town baths
came the sound of cheerful singing. Spring was certainly
in the air.

A smart yellow chariot, pulled by two white horses,
bowled over the stones of the main street. The driver,
proud of his carriage, shouted at the people to get out of
his way, while two or three stray dogs yapped and
snapped at the flying hooves.

Down by the town fountain sat Clement, a big muscular Briton. He scowled as he heard the chariot approaching; perhaps this was the same Roman sprig who had flicked a whip at him the day before.

He reached down to the ground, scooped up a handful of thick mud and then, as the chariot rattled past, he swung his arm quickly. There was a satisfying smacking noise and Clement saw a splodge of black spreading over the back of the gleaming white Roman tunic.

'Hm,' he thought, 'that was a good shot. Perhaps I could have made my living as an athlete.'

In his imagination Clement saw a vast, circular arena, packed with cheering spectators who were shouting in chorus the name of the great discus thrower.

'Cle-ment! Cle-ment!' cheered the crowd. Down on the sandy floor the handsome athlete scooped up the round metal disc, whirled gracefully on his sandalled feet and sent it soaring through the air. It curved upwards and a great cry went up as it was seen to fall way beyond the mark of Clement's nearest rival.

'Cle-ment! Cle-ment!' roared the crowd again, as a wreath of laurel leaves was placed on the brow of the mighty victor.

But Clement's daydream ended with a start. The chariot had wheeled in a cloud of dust and was on its way back towards him, the young driver shouting angrily. Clement did not wait; he took to his heels and disappeared down the maze of narrow town streets.

After a while he stopped running as he was sure that he had lost his pursuer in the crowded alleys. He looked around him, and saw that he was in front of a shop selling cool drinks. They looked delicious but Clement had no money.

Clement licked his dry lips. 'If I had a job,' he thought, 'I would drink until it came out of my ears. I wonder if I could get money by inventing and selling a new kind of drink. Then people would come from all over the province to buy from me.'

In his imagination Clement saw himself. He sat at the
top of some steps leading up to a white villa with tall
columns at the front. A line of Romans in long togas
stretched away into the distance. All of them were waving
bags of money and crying out in hoarse voices, 'Tell us
the way you make the drink, O Clement. There's gold if
you will tell us!'

But the daydream faded and there was only a dusty
street and a thirsty man without a job. Clement licked his
lips again and wandered on.

Now he was in the poorest quarter of the town. Just as
he was walking alongside a high brick wall a gate in it
burst open and a body was flung out to land with a thud
in the gutter at Clement's feet. The body yelled and
cursed as it hit the floor.

'And don't come back, you lazy dog!' roared a loud voice with a thick Roman accent.

Clement now saw a brawny man in a leather apron standing in the gateway, dusting his hands together. The body in the road struggled to its feet and slouched away, shouting something over its shoulder.

Clement was about to walk on when the brawny man spoke to him.

'Hey, you, Briton,' said the man. Clement stopped. 'Come here. You look half-starved to me, yet you seem to have good muscles for one of your weakly race. What's your trade if you've got one?'

Clement thought swiftly. There might be some profit here if he was careful about what he said. 'What's yours?' he asked in return.

'I am a master tile-maker and an artist in mosaics.'

Clement found it easy to lie. 'That's strange,' he said, 'I too am a maker of tiles by trade.'

A huge hand settled on his shoulder. 'Amazing,' said the man. 'It just so happens that I need a worker since the last one resigned. You can start right away.'

Clement's imagination was fired. He dreamed of becoming a master tile-maker in a purple toga, with a purse full of coins. In front of him hundreds of workmen slaved away while he gave orders to them and occasionally painted a delicate flower on glazed tiles.

Clement came to earth with a bump. The ham-like hand had pushed him swiftly inside the gate and was holding out a very heavy shovel.

'You can start by loading that barrow with clay,' said the master-tiler. 'My name is Maximus, but you can call me Sir.'

Clement thought the shovel and the barrow and the clay looked like very hard work, and he was tempted to run but then he thought of his empty pockets, sighed and set to work.

The job was certainly hard but it was not difficult. Clement worked alongside four other men and they all filled the barrows and then shovelled clay into square wooden tile-moulds, dusted over with sand to stop sticking.

A thin strip of wood had to be drawn over the full moulds to flatten and smoothe the clay and they were then put out to dry in the open air. As the day wore on the yard began to be filled with row after row of moulds.

Maximus strode up and down the rows lightly touching the clay in the moulds with the tips of his fingers.

'What's he doing?' grunted Clement to a little old man who was working near him.

'Testing them for dryness,' said the other. 'When they're nearly dry they go under cover to finish off.'

Maximus bawled at Clement. 'Hey, you! The great British tile-maker! Come over here! Turn this little lot out and stack them in the drying-shed.'

'Which ones do you mean?' asked Clement, looking at the rows of tiles. He did not want to make a mistake.

'Just the ones with the Emperor's name stamped on them.'

That did worry Clement. He had never been taught to read so how would he be able to recognize the Emperor's name? He inspected the tiles close to him. Some of them had patterns on them, some had marks which looked as if they might be written words. Clement scratched his head. If only he had been taught how to read!

In his imagination he saw himself as a fine-looking old man, a teacher, surrounded by books and scrolls. Carefully but quickly he was writing words on a wax tablet with a gold stylus, while at the same time he read aloud from a book to a group of admiring students.

'Hey, you! Dreamer!' It was Maximus again. 'Get on with it!'

Clement stooped and picked up a tile. It said 'MAX' on it. He turned the mould upside down and the clay fell out and splattered all over the floor. Maximus roared with anger.

'Fool!' he yelled. 'I said the ones with the Emperor's name on. That one's got my name on it. Look — MAX for Maximus. How long have I been the Emperor?'

Clement picked up another. This one had 'NER CAE' scratched on it.

'That's better, man. "Nero. Caesar." That's what it says.' A huge forefinger stabbed at Clement. 'Are you sure you are a tiler? All tilers are taught how to read and write by their masters. Can't you read?'

'Sorry, sir. Just a mistake because I was nervous. I could read and write before I made my first tile.' That was true anyway since he had never made a tile in his life.

Somehow he managed to sort out all the right tiles, but before long he was in trouble again. Maximus fairly went purple in the face when he found that his new workman had placed the drying tiles flat on top of each other so that they would all stick together.

'Tile-maker?' he shouted. 'You're never a tile-maker! But I'll give you one last chance. Just stoke the fires under the kilns and watch the doors of this shed while I am away. Even an idiot should be able to do that.'

Clement fed the fires under the huge square kilns until the sweat ran down his face and bare chest. A dog wandered in at the gate and ran towards the drying room and Clement flicked a lump of clay to send it howling out into the street again. The heat was terrible.

Over in the corner of the yard was a large tub of clean water for drinking. Clement walked over to it and plunged his heated face up to the neck in the cool, clear water. That felt better.

He cupped his hands and drank noisily, then squatted down in the shade of the tub for a rest.

The water had tasted good, but it would have been even better if there had been a pool there for a swim.

Clement daydreamed, and saw himself as a rich man visiting the town baths. He lay on a cool, stone slab while a slave poured oil on his body and then scraped the dirt away with a curved strigil. After that he ran lightly to the edge of a marble bath and plunged into the deep water, leaving a trail of bubbles behind him and gasping at the coldness.

The dream ended with a real gasp. Somebody had thrown a bucket of water over him as he squatted there. Of course it was Maximus.

'Get up!' yelled the tile-master. 'Look at the damage you have caused. The kiln fires have gone down so far that all the tiles inside have cooled too quickly and cracked!'

'I'm sorry,' said Clement. 'I was just . . .'

'And look at the drying-shed! I told you to watch the doors!'

He caught Clement by the ear and dragged him over to the shed. There were the neat rows of drying tiles. But to his horror, Clement saw that the dog must have come back while he was dreaming, for there were paw-marks all over a large number of the tiles.

Clement sighed. He turned towards Maximus just as the tile-master reached out a pair of brawny arms for him. The arms picked him up and lifted him high in the air.

For a second or two Clement started to dream what it would be like to be a great wrestler so that he could fight back. But then there was a huge crash and he sprawled full-length in the street outside the factory gates.

'Lie there!' shouted Maximus. 'You should be good at that. I've never known a liar like you!' The gates banged shut and Clement could hear the tile-master guffawing at his own joke.

Clement made his way back to the fountain in the town square. 'One of these days,' he thought, 'I shall have a really good job. . .'

He began to dream, and as he dreamed he slept.

The seal in the forest

Richard II's reign

That summer of 1381 was hot. The only cool place in the village was at the edge of the woods, and Anne, daughter of Thomas the Weaver, had made for herself a special hidden den under a great oak tree.

There she had found bramble bushes growing in a perfect circle with a small grassy space in the middle. She had burrowed patiently under the thorny, trailing branches, leaving no tracks behind her, and she knew that only she and the summer flies ever went there.

On the hottest day of the year that secret place was cool. Anne crawled carefully in and sat comfortably in the dappled shade to examine what she called her 'treasures'. These were a small collection of bits and pieces, all carefully wrapped in a piece of scarlet cloth, the remains of a petticoat which had been a present from her godmother.

Anne unrolled the cloth and smoothed it out on the grass. Then she picked her treasures up one by one.

First there was half of a broken wishbone from the Christmas goose: she knew that would bring her luck one day.

Then there was part of a gilded buckle which she had found lying near the edge of the highway: she rubbed it on her sleeve to make it shine.

There was the stump of a fat candle, given to her by the priest one day when she had helped him put new rushes on the church floor before Mass.

There was a rather smelly rabbit's foot, another good luck charm, which old Maggie-by-the-Mill had said a spell over. And now, today, there was yet another treasure to add to her collection, the best one yet. She dug deep into the pocket of her smock and laid her new find on the scarlet cloth.

It was a heavy, round object, about the size of Anne's hand and a little thicker than one of her mother's griddle-cakes. It seemed to be made of metal, but Anne did not think that it could be very precious because it did not glitter. Rather it was dull and tarnished.

She screwed up her eyes to try to make out a sort of picture or design that was raised on the flat top of the object. She could see what looked like the outline of a four-leaved clover and inside that a picture of a knight's coat-of-arms and shield. Above that was a knight's helmet and on top of that some sort of animal. She wished she knew what it was.

As Anne examined the object she noticed something stuck to it near the animal's head. She used her finger-nail to ease out a tiny flake of red wax, perhaps part of a candle. But that did not help her at all.

She started and sat motionless as the sound of a twig snapping came from outside her den. Then she relaxed as she heard the steady rasping sound of a deer cropping the grass at the edge of the forest.

She thought about the previous day when she had found her latest treasure. She had been sent by her father with a piece of cloth which he had just woven for the castle.

Just as she neared the big gates a group of horsemen had swept past her and into the castle yard. Their faces had been grimy with dust and their horses sweating. Anne had had to screw herself into the side of the track to escape the flying hooves, and, teetering on the edge of the ditch she had almost been hit by something flying through the air. That thing was her new treasure.

She scratched out another flake of red wax and then, still puzzled, she rolled up her scarlet bundle and stuffed it back into a narrow hole she had made under the oak tree's roots.

Outside the den there was a quick movement and the sound of the deer's hooves scudding away across the turf. Then she heard men's voices and lay still to listen.

'Sit here a minute, Hal,' said one voice, that of a man puffing breathlessly. 'This wind's as hot as if it were blowing from the miller's oven. Sit down, lad, there's little you can do for now.'

Another voice replied, lighter and younger, and Anne recognized it as that of a young man whom she had seen once or twice in the forest. He usually wore the livery of the Duke of Lancaster, and he carried a longbow. She supposed that his job was to look after the game in the woods and to scare away vagabonds and outlaws.

Once he had spoken kindly to her when he had found her gathering acorns for the family pig. He had started to explain that everything in the forest, even the acorns, belonged to his master, the Duke, and that really she was stealing. At that she had taken fright and backed off, scattering the acorns from her apron as she turned and bolted for her cottage home.

The young man spoke again. 'Old John'll want his game,' he said. 'While you sit there making the heather wet with your sweat, there might be a band of outlaws stealing deer.'

The older man laughed scornfully. 'Outlaws? Stealing his deer? There's plenty in the village who would say that they have as much right to hunt and eat deer as has John of Gaunt, Duke of Lancaster!'

'Hush, you old fool!' snapped the young man. 'I know the law. The law is made by the strongest man. My master owns thirty castles, has a thousand men-at-arms and could send three times a thousand arrows singing through this hot air into your flabby flesh! If he says that he owns the deer, then who are we to argue?'

Anne heard the older man struggling to his feet, still grumbling. 'Oh come on, then,' he said. 'We'll walk over by the small pool. I saw a heap of wild boar droppings there yesterday.'

Their voices died away, but as they did so Anne thought she heard the younger one say, 'And keep your eyes open for the seal. . .'

That evening, as the family sat at their supper in the dying light of the day, Anne spoke to her father. He was sitting on a settle near to the open window, looking tired and worried. His appetite had been poor, and Anne was hoping that the piece of rabbit pie which was still on his plate might come her way.

'Father', she said. 'Has the Duke, John of Gaunt, got a lot of land?'

Her father grunted. 'More than he should have,' he said grumpily.

'Does he own all our forest?'

'He says he does.' This reminded him of something, and he turned to his wife, Anne's mother. 'Is there any news of neighbour Seth?'

'It is as we thought,' sniffed Anne's mother. 'Sir Hugh is the magistrate and he is liegeman to the Duke. Seth was found hunting deer in the Duke's forest close to Sir Hugh's castle. Sir Hugh's men caught him and locked him in the castle cellars. I daresay he will stay there now until they hang him!'

'Why don't they chop his hands off?' asked Anne curiously. 'Will-by-the-Stream says that's what they do with people who are caught stealing in some places.'

Anne's father's face became angry. 'And I say it was not stealing, young miss! You should talk less to that fellow Will. There are some of us in this village who are thinking of changing things round here just now!'

'What do you mean? What will you change?' asked Anne, but her father would say no more. His face took on an angry scowl and he threw the left-over rabbit pie to the dog. So Anne got no more food, neither did she get the chance to ask him the question she had really wanted answered.

However, later that night, as she climbed under the woollen blankets on her bed she called out to her older brother as he sat carving away at a love-spoon for his sweetheart.

'Edward?'

'Go to sleep, child. It's late.'

'Edward, what is a seal?'

'Seal? Why, everyone knows that. A seal is a kind of huge fish-creature which lives in the cold seas. Don't you remember Harald coming from the Norse lands last summer with his furs and sealskins? He told me how they hunted seals from their boats with short throwing spears.'

'Are there any of these seals in our forest, Edward?'

'In the forest? Haven't I just told you that they live in the sea? Now go to sleep and stop asking stupid questions!'

Anne turned over to sleep, wondering about Edward's answers. If seals lived in the sea, how could the two foresters have been keeping their eyes open for one near her den?

Anne had a restless night. She dreamed of seals and of the dungeons where their neighbour was being kept prisoner. In the middle of the night she woke up and heard men's voices in the cottage, her father's one of them. They were talking seriously, in low tones, and Anne fell asleep again after hearing them mention London and a name like Tyler or Taylor.

Later on still she half-woke again when a very strong voice was chanting a rhyme she fancied she had heard before:

'When Adam delved and Eve span,
Who was then the gentleman?'

The next morning proved to be bright with a hot sun rising quickly to burn off the white mist from the water-meadows. Anne was rather surprised to see her father's loom standing idle in the corner of the room — often by that time he was hard at work.

'Where's Father?' she asked.

'Off on a fool's errand,' said her mother shortly. 'If you have a prayer to say, then say one today. Pray that he comes back safely. No, better still, pray that he falls down and breaks his leg before he and his foolish friends get out of this village. That way he will never get to London at all.'

'London?' said Anne, excited. 'Is Father going to London? Will he see the King?'

'Hush your prattle, child, and get off out of the house. I've said too much already. Off you go now, while I clear up the mess they left last night.' And she made such a bustle that Anne was glad to grab a crust of bread and run off to the forest where she sat in her den to think about all the strange happenings of the last twenty-four hours.

As she sat there she became aware of shouting and crashing some way off in the forest. Then there came a loud scream, of a man in pain, and soon the sound of approaching footsteps. Anne lay in her den, her heart beating fast. The footsteps stopped outside, and she heard a man say quietly, 'He's dead, I tell you, dead as a doornail.'

Another voice said, 'Aye, slit from knee to breast by the tusks of that boar. I never saw such a monstrous brute round here before.'

More voices joined in, and Anne, peering through the brambles, saw a small group of men, some kneeling at the side of a man who was lying on the grass, some standing looking down. There was blood on the clothing of the injured man. Close by lay the body of a huge bristly boar, transfixed by a wooden spear, its head pointing curved tusks skywards.

'What's to be done, then?' said a strong voice, and with a start Anne realized that it was her father speaking. 'We shall never get to London at this rate.'

'Don't talk like that,' said another. 'I'm going, whatever happens. I don't believe Jack is dead, but he needs help. Here, you two, take him back to his wife, and mind you tell her that it was an accident with a spear. She's got a sharp tongue and a loose one, has that woman, and we don't want her telling everybody that her husband got half-killed poaching the Duke's wild boar!'

Two men lifted the injured man carefully and carried him away, while the rest set to work to skin the dead animal and cut it into joints. They thrust the still-steaming flesh into their pouches and bags.

The remains of the boar were flung into a clump of bushes out of sight, and some attempt was made to clear the mess from the grass where they had been working. Anne's father was still unhappy, however.

'Perhaps we ought not to go after all,' he said. 'Suppose Jack's accident is an omen of bad luck.'

'Call yourself a man?' said the leader scornfully. 'I don't believe in omens, and Wat Tyler and a hundred thousand others are waiting for me. You can stay behind if you like but nothing will stop me going! Was all our talk in your cottage the other night just a waste of time? Are you content to let the Duke and others like him treat us as slaves, or shall we rebel with Wat Tyler and either win our freedom or die in the attempt?' His voice had risen as he spoke.

Anne's father raised his hand as if to argue, but at that moment the whole group stiffened in fear. Far away Anne heard the wail of a hunting horn and the thud of horses' hooves. It was a hunting party from the castle, and by the sound of it, it was heading straight for the spot where the men were standing.

The men moved swiftly. The boar's remains were
dragged out of the bushes and one of the group ran with
them into the forest, dragging the skin along the floor to
set a trail. All the others slipped away into the shadows,
except for Thomas, who stood, feet firmly planted, to wait
for the hunters. If Anne had reached out from where she
was hiding she could have touched his feet.

She heard the cries of the huntsmen and then the baying of hounds. For a minute or two all was confusion, with shouts and crashing of horses and dogs yelping as they were whipped into order. A smell of horse-sweat and leather was everywhere.

When she dared to peep out again, Anne saw her father standing arguing with a large huntsman in a leather jerkin. Men on horseback filled the clearing, and two servants were keeping the dogs from following the trail laid by the boar-skin.

'I tell you I know of no unlawful hunting!' said Thomas firmly.

The man in leather sneered. 'What, blood here on the grass, everything flattened down, blood on your own arm, man?' Anne saw that there was a smear of blood on her father's wrist.

Thomas rubbed the smear, thinking quickly. 'I — er — I scratched myself on a bramble when I was looking to see what was in the bushes. I thought I could see something,' he said.

'Aye, thought you saw the Duke's deer, no doubt. He'll have your head for this, fellow!'

'But I have killed no deer,' said Thomas. 'Look, I was standing here for a rest from my walk. I am an honest weaver. I paused here, as I said to rest, when I caught sight of something in this bush. I reached down into the bramble to find out what it was, and as I did so I scratched myself.'

Thomas pushed his hand into the bramble bush, trying to scratch himself deliberately to cover up the smear of blood. With a sudden flash of inspiration, Anne, hiding in that very bush pushed her strange 'treasure', the one with the picture on, into her father's open hand. Thomas, with a cry of surprise drew out his hand and said, 'Look! See! This must be what I saw.'

'What is it?' said the huntsman, peering down, and
then gave a great cry of excitement. 'Man! Do you know
what you have found? Why man, it must be your lucky
day. Old John will certainly reward you and us for this!'

'What is it, then?' said Thomas, peering at the thing in
his hand.

'It's old John's great seal, man! Lost the other day by
his secretary as he brought it up from London to the castle.
See, there is the Duke's coat of arms. He presses the seal
on hot wax to seal his letters. Quick, we must get back. He
is due to ride off to Scotland today, and we must get this to
him before he goes.'

Within seconds Anne's father was hoisted up on to a
horse, behind one of the riders, and the whole party swept
off out of the forest towards the castle.

It was quite late that evening when Thomas came
home again, grinning from ear to ear and his breath
smelling sweetly of wine. He was swinging a sack in his
hand, and as he stumbled over the threshold he gave his
wife and Anne a huge bear-hug of delight.

'What a day!' he said. 'Do you know, wife, that I have spoken with old John of Gaunt himself.' He told the whole story of what had happened in the wood, finishing up by saying, '. . . and just at that moment, providence made my fingers grasp that precious object!' Anne kept very quiet at that point, but her father went straight on with his story.

'Then when we came to the castle,' he said, 'my Lord the Duke was so overjoyed to see his great seal again that he patted my shoulder and gave me wine in a silver cup. Yes, in a silver cup, no less! And see, what else he made his servants fetch for me.'

Anne's father emptied the sack on to the rough table and out tumbled a joint of meat, five round loaves, and three fat fish with silver scales.

'And that's not all! See!' He opened his fist and there was a coin made of dull yellow metal. 'Gold, wife! Gold! See, Anne, this is what gold looks like.' And as Anne and her mother looked at the coin, he said, 'And that's still not all. Old John says that I may weave cloth for the castle for the rest of my life!'

Thomas's wife wept for joy. 'It was God's will that you should not go to London,' she said. 'It was his will that you should leave all such things to those poor men with no jobs. Honest weavers like you should not be mixed up in their struggles.'

For a moment Thomas was silent. Then he gave a little sigh and nodded. 'Perhaps you're right. But I should like to have seen London and to have marched with Wat Tyler. He will do great things and we shall have stirring news before long. However, as for me, as you say, God willed that I should find the Duke's seal and stay at home.'

Anne said nothing, and in fact it was many, many years before she told her father the truth about the events of that day.

'We were both disappointed on that day,' she said, when she finally told him her part in the story. 'You were rather disappointed at not being able to go to London — though as it turned out you might well have been killed if you had gone, along with that famous Wat Tyler you were always talking about — but I was disappointed for a simpler reason.'

She laughed as she remembered. 'You see, I was hoping against hope to catch a glimpse of one of those fish-creatures called seals. I thought there was one loose in the forest somewhere! I was very disappointed when the missing seal turned out to be nothing more than that rather dirty lump of metal I'd found by the roadside!'

The bow   *Medieval*

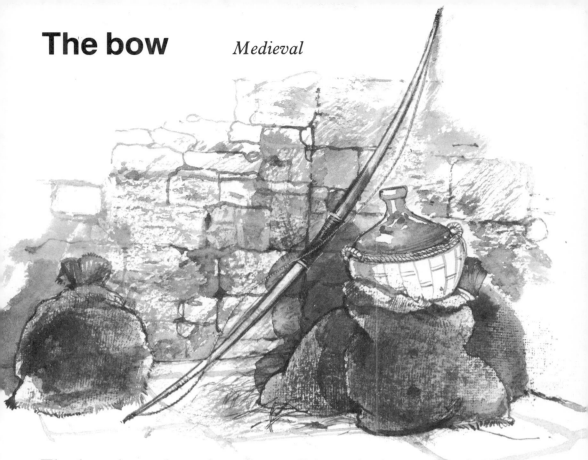

The bow leaned against the wall in a dark corner of the mill house kitchen. It had not been strung nor fired since Stephen's father, the miller, had broken his right arm repairing a split in one of the great mill-wheel paddles.

Occasionally Stephen would lift the bow from its corner and lovingly rub fresh goose-grease into the plaited cord, but he had never tried to bend it to string it. His father said whenever he saw him with it, 'That's a man's bow, son. Leave it there until you find a man's needs to go with it.'

And so the great bow stayed in its corner, gathering dust, while Stephen had to be content with smaller bows for play and practice.

By the time Stephen was fourteen years old he was as tall as his father, but as his mother often said to his shame, he carried little flesh on his bones. His muscles were strong enough, it is true, and he could heave flour sacks or drive the heavy ox-cart as well as any man at the mill, but he lacked the flesh to make him really strong.

So he took up wrestling, and because of his height and gangling arms he proved an awkward opponent. For a long time he was thrown and pinned, got up and was thrown again, but quite often he won his bout by skill and brains.

Gradually his shoulders broadened and his chest deepened. His thighs became thick and heavy from all the lifting he did and so the time came when he was able to wrestle with the best and win most of his fights. When he reached his sixteenth birthday he was ready to take on any man in the district at catch-and-throw.

On the eve of the feast of St. John the Baptist the following year, Stephen's father sent him with the cart to take flour to the village priest. Stephen yoked up the two black oxen to the clumsy mill cart, and drove it, creaking, down the rutted lane from the mill to the church barn. The oxen flicked their tails at the flies, and the dust blowing up from the road made Stephen's eyes sore.

The tithe barn was high-beamed and cool. Spears of sunlight leaned down from the air-holes at the top of the walls and golden grains of dust hung in them. Stephen humped in the sacks of flour from the cart and then went on one knee at the priest's feet to receive his blessing.

48

'Thank you, Father,' he said rising and making the sign of the cross. He brushed loose straw from his knees and was about to go, but the priest stopped him.

'How old are you now, Stephen?'

'Sixteen, Father. Seventeen at Michaelmas, God willing.'

'Hm. Sixteen. Old enough to serve the King and Church in the wars in France?'

Stephen was surprised. 'I have not thought of such a thing, Father. The mill is my life, and I am needed there.'

The priest patted him on the shoulder. 'Quite right, of course. Honour thy father and thy mother.'

'My father still thinks of me as a boy, anyway,' said Stephen.

'Our king was but a boy when he first fought in battle. Our Lord Bishop has blessed the war King Henry fights, and we all pray for his endeavours. But prayers alone will not win battles. Think about it, boy.'

Stephen did think about it as he drove back through the village. He remembered a talk he had had with a one-armed traveller who had called at the mill early in the summer to beg bread and water. The man had been wounded in the French wars and was full of stories.

The man talked of the crossbow, of the incredible speed of the bolt and its straight flight. But his eyes lit up when he told stories of the English longbow and the men who used it.

One of his stories was of how he had seen a man on horseback struck by an arrow from a longbow which went through the armour on his thigh, through the thick leather of the saddle and into the horse, killing the beast stone dead.

'They came from Wales, you know, lad,' he had said, talking of the great bows. 'That is, the first ones did. And some say the Welsh archers are still the best and the strongest. But what a weapon! What a weapon!' His eyes grew dim as he looked down at the swinging sleeve where once there had been an arm. Like Stephen's father he would never fire the longbow again.

By the village green Stephen's cart was stopped by
two of his friends, Rob and John, both younger by a year
than he was. Stephen slackened the leads and the oxen
turned to graze at the long grass by the side of the road.
Stephen told his friends what the priest had said to him.

'I wish I could go,' said Rob regretfully. 'This village
holds nothing for me. Nothing but work, that is, from
sunrise to sunset.'

'Me too,' said John. 'I used to look forward to
Sundays, but since they have stopped us playing ball-
games, life is very dull.'

'My father says that the law is right. Archery practice is more important than football,' said Stephen.

'All fathers are like that,' said Rob with a groan. 'It may be more important but it's not such fun. Oh, I wish I were your age, Stephen, I should be away to France to fight with the King tomorrow.'

Stephen laughed. 'So you would,' he said. 'So you would. You were always mad-headed. But cheer up, tomorrow is John the Baptist's day and no work for anyone. There will be wrestling, they say.'

'Yes,' said John. 'There will be wrestling. And archery. Always wrestling and archery. When are we going to get back to having a match of football against the next village again? That was a real game!'

Stephen nodded. He remembered the last game when a ball made out of a pig's bladder stuffed with straw was fought over by scores of men and boys. He remembered it more as a battle than a game, with plenty of chance to pay off old scores and private fights going on all day. No, if he were given the choice he would have wrestling rather than football — it was less dangerous.

Their chatter was interrupted by a commotion at the other side of the village green, where a small cluster of people had gathered round a bearded man who was speaking forcefully. As the three friends drew nearer they could tell by his speech that he was a stranger to that area.

'Now friends,' said the man. 'I beg you to have nothing to do with the man who comes tomorrow calling himself the Champion of all England. He is a wrestler to

beat all. At St. Bartholomew's Fair in Clerkenwell last
year he killed two men, both brothers and sons of a
franklin from near there. Killed them stone dead he did.
Both died of cracked skulls and broken backs.'

The little crowd murmured, and the boys smiled. They
had heard stories like that before.

Often, when a fair was due, a wrestler would send a
man to the village where he was to fight, to tell stories
such as the one they had just heard. This had two
purposes. First of all, it attracted the curious who came to
gape at a man who had killed others at the sport.
Secondly, it sometimes had the effect of scaring off
challengers, who didn't fancy getting a broken neck.
Thus the 'champion' had more chance of winning all the
prizes and bets.

'What is his name, this mighty man?' called out Stephen. Then, before the man could answer, Rob shouted 'Goliath!' and John called 'Samson!'

The crowd sniggered. But the bearded man pushed his way roughly towards the three friends. Now that he was closer they could see that he was dark, sun-burned, and hard-looking. He carried a dagger with a well-worn handle at his belt. His grey eyes were as cold as northern ice.

'Big words from small boys, I see,' said the man contemptuously. 'But then perhaps you will be among the challengers tomorrow when Yngram Twynham — note the name, friends — Champion of all England, strides on to this green. I daresay the three of you together might last ten seconds!' He turned his back on them, and then said over his shoulder, 'That is, provided that Yngram has one hand tied behind his back!'

The boys smarted at his words. The man addressed the villagers again. 'Stay away from Yngram Twynham, friends. He would fell that ox of a boy over there, just as he felled the prize bull of Sir Edward Coke, with one blow of his fist!'

Stephen shrugged his shoulders and turned away. He had no wish to quarrel with this man, although he felt his face going red with anger. As they went the boys were followed by the man's loud laughter and not a few guffaws from the crowd.

That evening, before sunset, Stephen took his father's old bow out of its corner and went outside into the mill-yard. He ran the greased cord through his fingers and

then with a quick stoop and a lithe movement he slipped the cord's loop over the end of the wood. The bow seemed to come alive as it bent and the taut cord twanged roundly and sweetly.

Stephen slipped a horn bracer on to his left wrist to protect it from the slap of the cord. Then he fitted the nock of a goose-feather arrow on to the cord and raised the bow.

The wood creaked softly as the arrow was drawn back, back, back until the angle of the cord touched Stephen's lips. His eye selected a target, a sturdy wooden post over by the mill-pond, well-scarred from previous practice with smaller bows. Then, humming like an angry bee, the arrow flew through the air and struck the post with a splintering thud.

Stephen walked over to pull out the arrow. The old bow was as sound as his father had always said it was, for the arrow had gone through the oak post so hard that most of it was sticking out on the far side. Only the goose flights had stopped it from going right through all the way.

Stephen held the bow out at arm's length. Now he knew that he could use it and use it well. Something big was stirring at the back of his mind, an idea that he was refusing to let take shape yet. For the moment he went back into the house and put the bow back into its corner.

The next day was disappointing at first for a light rain fell from scudding grey clouds. The villagers who had been looking forward to the festivities of the holy day waited miserably for the rain to clear. But then, at midday, the grey clouds blew away and a pale sun shone.

Several of the villagers lit the first of the great John the Baptist fires. They had been prepared for a long time from clean wood and bones, and although the rain had wet the wood, it was not long before first smoke and then flames came from the pile. The smell of the burning bones was foul, but it was traditional to build the fires so, and the village children, wrinkling their noses at the stench, remembered the story of how long ago a fire of bones had frightened away dragons.

Stephen, Rob, and John sauntered across the green to where preparations for the wrestling were going on. The so-called champion had arrived. He was a big man with a barrel-shaped chest and knotted muscles, but Stephen, watching carefully, noted that there was a streak of grey in his short hair, and one leg seemed shorter than the other. The champion was getting old and had had earlier injuries. Perhaps this was the year that he would be beaten by a younger man.

They wandered on to the archery competition where a match was taking place between longbow and crossbow. The longbowman shot rapidly and accurately, his clothyard arrows curving through the air to cluster in the straw target round the golden bull's-eye. His movements were graceful and rhythmic, and the watchers were applauding every shot.

The crossbowman sat on a tuft of grass with a short bolt tucked under his chin while the string was drawn back on the bow. Then he dropped the bolt into the smooth groove, raised the bow and fired. The bolt slid through the air at an incredible speed, straight and true and thumped into the straw, burying itself almost completely with the power of the shot.

The competition was fierce, and the crossbowman won. His shots never seemed to vary. But the crowd preferred the longbow and were disappointed.

Stephen snorted. 'Competition is one thing. Actual fighting is another. My father says that longbows win battles because of the speed of re-loading. He says that King Harry will have only a few crossbows in his army but over a thousand longbows.'

He thought of the great bow in the mill kitchen and the idea he had had the night before stirred again. He remembered the stories of the one-armed beggar and the words of the priest at the tithe barn.

His thoughts were interrupted, however, by a shout from the wrestling. The champion had just thrown a young man who now lay groaning on the short turf, face twisted in agony and hands clutched to his ribs. The champion picked up a wet rag and wiped his face, then called out, 'Anyone else want to get his neck broken or shall I take the prize now?'

Stephen looked at the man on the ground. He recognized him as a freeman with a big family who needed him to keep them in food and shelter. He hoped that there was no serious injury. Wrestling which ended with a man groaning like that usually meant there had been foul play and dirty tricks. That might well be another sign that the champion was getting old.

The man on the ground groaned as friends carried him away, and that decided Stephen. Swiftly he slipped out of his leather belt and stripped off his jerkin. The crowd went silent as he stepped forward to face Yngram Twynham.

The champion threw down the wet rag and sneered. 'A boy?' he snapped. 'Is that the best this village can do?' But in spite of the words his shrewd eyes noted Stephen's solid frame and brawny arms, and he turned to whisper to the bearded man who had been talking about him the day before. The man looked over at Stephen and scowled.

Stephen walked round the grassy clearing and stooped to pick up a rough stone, half-hidden by the turf. Such a stone might have got there accidentally, but could easily have been dropped on purpose: to land on that would be to suffer a nasty bruise. He hurled the stone away over the heads of the crowd and heard it splash into the pond. Then he faced the champion, lowered his head and raised his arms, waiting for him to attack.

Twynham circled twice warily and then came in with a rush, fingers out towards Stephen's eyes, and hoping for a quick throw. Stephen dodged the fingers and closed, feeling a sudden pain in his foot as the man stamped on his instep. The fingers dug sharp nails into the flesh of his shoulders and in spite of himself he winced.

Well, now he knew what he had to face — dirty tricks all the way. He smiled to himself — such tricks might make some lose their temper and their concentration, but he had been more or less ready for them.

As Twynham pushed forward, arms locked, Stephen leaned backwards and sideways, at the same time releasing his grasp. The champion went off balance and almost fell. Stephen stepped back. The crowd sniggered.

Twynham circled again, his face pale now and then suddenly lunged out with his foot at the boy's kneecap. But Stephen stepped lightly out of the way and then, before the champion could move again, he moved into the lock position once more.

At these close quarters there was less chance of a flying kick or a gouge from fingers, but Stephen was not prepared for the sudden sharp blow in the pit of his stomach as the champion raised his knee viciously. The two wrestlers swayed as the blow went home, but one blow like that had little effect.

Stephen shifted his grip slightly to get in even closer and tried putting weight on the man's left side, the side where he had noticed the hint of a lame leg. A grunt of pain told him that he had guessed right in thinking there might be weakness there. He bore down again and felt Twynham beginning to go.

Then suddenly he received a violent, shattering butt in the face from the champion's grizzled skull. Blood spurted from his nose and he thought he could also feel a gash in his cheek. The blood ran into his mouth and tasted salt. The man's grinning face seemed to swim before his eyes, but he hung on with all his strength. He felt the knee come up into his stomach again, and nausea gagged in his throat.

The crowd's angry shouts revived him and slowly his head cleared. He had not released his hold on Twynham's shoulders in spite of the pain, and now he spat blood and tried a trick of his own. He gave a deep groan and rolled his eyes as if he were losing consciousness, at the same

time slackening his grip slightly and giving a little at the knees. He looked up at the champion's dark eyes and saw triumph there. He let his knees bend even more, and then as the champion pressed, he suddenly straightened up, twisted violently and put all his strength into a great heave on the man's weak side.

Twynham's pressure turned into a despairing clutch, but it was too late. Stephen's heave had him off balance, his weak leg gave way and with a huge thump he hit the turf. He screamed as pain shot through his body. Stephen fastened his weight over the man and pinned him down.

Even then the champion tried to butt the boy in the face again, but Stephen easily avoided the blow and pressed his shoulder into the man's throat so that he choked for breath. The crowd cheered. The bout was over.

Later, after all the congratulations were done with, Stephen was surprised to see the champion coming over to him. He was limping slightly but he shrugged when the boy asked about his leg.

'I came over to thank you,' he said gruffly, and his eyes looked sad all of a sudden. 'The leg was broken last year, and you could, if you had wished, have broken it again today. The crowd would not have thought ill of you had you done so. You are a good lad. No, you're a good man, for you are a lad no more.'

Stephen could not feel friendly towards the man he had defeated. 'You play dirty, master Twynham,' he said shortly. 'Your foul tricks bring good men to ruin. I ought to have broken your leg.'

Twynham laughed. 'It's all part of the game,' he said. 'Now that you're a man you'll learn that soon enough.' He walked away whistling.

Suddenly Stephen knew what he wanted to do. His mind went back to the old bow at the mill and his fingers itched to feel it again. Without looking around he picked up his belt and jerkin and slung them over his shoulder. Over at the edge of the green the boys were kindling the last bonfire of the day, and smoke and sparks were flying up into the evening air. But Stephen did not stop. His boyhood was over and ahead of him lay other things.

Girls don't go on the stage

Tudor

Christopher and Catherine were twins. As babies they were as alike as two peas in a pod and even when they were eleven years old they were still very much alike — so much so, that if Catherine had dressed up in Christopher's clothes she could have been mistaken for him. They both had long, fair hair and blue eyes, and they were both tall for their age.

The twins' father, Francis Jackson, was a wool merchant from Boston in Lincolnshire. He had built up a good business and owned a fine, timbered house in the main street of the town.

Christopher and Catherine were brought up well: they could read and write, thanks to lessons from a private tutor, and they could play quite tunefully on both the viol and the recorder. They were just beginning dancing lessons from a visiting French dancing-master when suddenly their mother was taken ill.

The illness was not severe, but it was bad enough for the doctor to visit the house every day. Christopher and Catherine were no help and were often in the way so their father decided that they would have to go away for a while, until their mother recovered.

Francis looked at his two children as they stood in front of him in the dark-beamed sitting room.

'My dears,' he said, smiling at them, 'I think that you would enjoy visiting your Aunt Mary in London. She has a pleasant house on Bankside and if you go there for about a month I think I can promise you two things. First of all you will enjoy your stay, for my sister Mary has no children of her own and so she will spoil you. Secondly, it will give you a chance to see our fine capital city of London.'

'Is mother so ill, then?' asked Catherine anxiously.

'No. Your mother is making good progress, but she needs to rest and be quiet, and nobody could say that this house is restful with you two around it! Now see that Martha packs your travelling bags and I will arrange for you to be escorted to London.'

Christopher packed his recorder, a fancy leather belt which his father had brought him back once from the Netherlands, and a set of five-stones.

Catherine packed her favourite rag doll, her gold brocade slippers, and a goose-quill writing pen.

They left the unimportant things like clothes to be packed by Martha, their serving maid. That worthy girl tut-tutted about the twins going all the way to London, warned them of the dangers of not washing behind their

ears, and sent them off with a smacking kiss on both cheeks.

The journey to London was long and tiring. Christopher and Catherine rode on two of their father's horses as far as Lincoln, and Jeremy the groom rode with them. Then, at Lincoln, they were taken into the family coach of some friends who were going to London. The journey took several days, stopping at night in strange towns, but it was tedious rather than exciting for the roads were hard and the horses slow.

At last the coach rumbled over London Bridge with its tall houses and shops slung over the muddy river. Tall-masted ships lay at anchor below the bridge and up and downstream the children could see watermen pulling their boats with steady strokes from one side of the Thames to the other.

Aunt Mary welcomed them noisily to her house on Bankside. She was a very cheerful soul with black laughing eyes and rich brown hair caught up in a knot at the back. She kissed them both soundly, thanked the people who had brought them and took them inside to hear the news from Lincolnshire.

'Now,' she said at last when the gossip was all done and they were sitting together on a high-backed oak settle. 'Here you are and here you stay for a month or so until your mother feels better. At the end of that time you will be real little Londoners, I'll be bound.'

The holiday went well right from the start. Aunt Mary had lots of interesting friends and the house was busy and cheerful the whole day through. Her own husband had been a sailor in the navy, a famous man who had lost his life for the Queen in the great battle of the Armada, and the house was full of curios brought from overseas.

A sailor's brass-bound telescope lay on the sill of the bow-window that looked over the river Thames. A gleaming cutlass hung from braided ribbons over the huge fireplace. Two iron cannon-balls stood in the hearth and a fine silk rug from Cathay lay on the polished stone slabs of the floor.

'You can have a look through dear Samuel's sea chest, if you like,' said Aunt Mary one day.

The chest was huge, big enough for them both to have sat in, and it was full of exciting things. There were bags of coloured sea shells, rolled-up parchment charts that crackled when the children handled them, leather purses jingling with strange foreign coins. Wrapped in paper were two long shawls from India and at the bottom of the chest lay a long, knotted camel-whip from Araby and a fearsome native axe from the New World. Everything in the chest smelled of salt and tar and musky spices.

Catherine and Christopher loved the sea chest and spent hours wrapping and unwrapping the things in it, wondering how Uncle Samuel had got them all.

But outside the summer sun shone down and the house began to get really hot in spite of the open shutters and doors. Soon the children began to want to spend more and more time out of doors.

Aunt Mary was very good. She took them for walks all round the old city so that they got used to the narrow, crowded streets and the broad river. They saw the big churches and the fine town houses of the rich.

They even went as far as the village of Richmond where their aunt said that the Queen was due to arrive on one of her 'Progresses'. But there they were disappointed: there were vast and jostling crowds, and all the twins managed to see were the heads of some of the Queen's courtiers and the golden tassels of the canopy they were carrying to shield her from the sun.

But the cheers of the crowd and the sight of all the boats decorated with flags made it a very exciting day in spite of their disappointment.

After three weeks they really seemed to have seen everything. One day, Christopher said to his aunt, 'Now that we have been out with you so much we are beginning to know our way around. Will you not let us go out by ourselves today?'

Aunt Mary was a sensible woman and she expected them to be sensible too. 'Very well,' she said, 'but stay out of the very narrow streets where there are a lot of vagabonds. And stay away from the deep river.'

The twins dashed off and went to their favourite spot by the river to watch the boats. Suddenly Christopher said, 'I'm going to go right down to the edge of the river, on to the mud. I've seen children picking things up and I might find something if I look hard.'

Catherine tucked up her skirts and they both slung their shoes round their necks. Soon they were paddling along in the thick mud by the water's edge. Not that they found much: Christopher collected a piece of carved and painted wood that might once have been part of a ship's figurehead. Catherine found a tiny silver coin with a hole in it which she thought would look well on a chain round her neck.

'What do you think this is?' asked Christopher after a while. He was looking up at a long, painted barge lying above the watermark, sheltered from the weather and the tides by a rough, shed-like building open at the end facing the river.

The children went into the boat-house and walked all round the barge. Then, feeling daring, they clambered up a rickety rotten ladder to stand on the deck.

It was certainly a barge of the sort used by important people which the twins had often seen being rowed by about twenty men. This one was in very good condition, all the paintwork fresh and the brass rails gleaming as if they had just been polished.

There was a raised platform at one end with a canopy over it, and below that a flight of steps led underneath the deck. Wandering down there the twins found two small cabins with glass windows. They pushed open the door of one of them and tiptoed in.

Catherine knelt on the purple cushions by the window and pretended to wave to an imaginary crowd.

'Look, Chris,' she said. 'I'm the Queen waving to the loyal subjects of her capital city.'

'Hm,' said her brother. 'You look more like a savage monkey in a cage gibbering at the gawping public!'

Suddenly Christopher grabbed Catherine's arm. Over their heads there was the sound of footsteps. The twins stood stock-still, feeling afraid. Then they heard men's voices, low at first and then getting louder.

'Well then,' said the one. 'Try me.'

'As you will,' said the other.

The footsteps started to do what seemed like a dance but then the dance stopped and there was the clash of steel and a curse. The dance started again, slower now, and the children realized that what they were listening to was the noise of a fight. Over their heads, up on deck, were two men fighting with swords!

Christopher was all for staying hidden until the fight was over, but Catherine was braver. She took her brother by the hand and urged him to follow her up the steps until they could see what was happening on deck.

There, on the raised platform above the cabin, two men in gaudy clothes were circling each other warily. Both held a drawn sword in one hand and a short dagger in the other.

First one would make a lunge which the other swerved away from, then the other would slash wildly, narrowly missing his opponent. Neither of them looked like fighting-men, however, for one was fairly old and very out of breath from carrying too much fat, while the other was so tall and skinny that his clothes just hung on him.

Catherine whispered in Christopher's ear, 'Wait until they really attack each other then make a dash for the ladder.'

But just at that moment the fight ended. The taller of the two, who had a spiky red beard, slashed above his opponent's head and then jabbed forward so that the point of his sword seemed to be going into the fat man's heart. But the fat man turned slightly, raised his arm so that the point went underneath it and gave out a ghastly yell.

Clutching the sword under his arm the fat man staggered about the deck groaning, and then at last collapsed on his back with a final ear-piercing shriek. The tall man raised his foot and put it on his chest, waved his hand in the air and said, 'So dies a treacherous coward!'

Catherine felt faint, but then she saw that the fat man was far from dead. As a matter of fact he appeared to be laughing, and suddenly the tall man was laughing too. Soon they were sitting side by side on the deck laughing fit to burst and holding on to each other in their mirth.

The twins smiled, and then giggled, and then could not help joining in and laughing as well. Instantly the fat man sprang to his feet, crying out, 'A rat! A rat! In the arras!'

'What,' said the thin man, seeing the children. 'Have we an audience here? Then bow, my master, bow.' And both men fell to one knee with a deep bow.

The twins did not know what to make of it all until Christopher said suddenly, 'Oh, I know, you are actors!'

The men bowed again. Actors they certainly were and soon they were all sitting on the boat's deck while the two men explained that they were rehearsing a scene from the historical play of 'Henry the Fifth' which was to be performed that night at the Globe Theatre, Bankside.

'Oh, can we come to see it?' asked Catherine. 'Please can we come?'

The red-bearded one looked doubtful. 'Plays are not for children,' he said. 'But, look, come round to the back of the theatre at seven this evening and I will take you in to stand at the side of the stage to see my great performance.'

He placed his hand on his heart and bowed. 'And now, fare thee well, young master and fair maid. Farewell.' He backed away, still bowing, while Catherine and Christopher laughed and clapped.

Aunt Mary was none too pleased. The twins' clothes were dirty, their feet were muddy, and now they were telling this tale of meeting actors and wanting to go to the theatre. However she was a kind-hearted woman and at last agreed that they might go.

'But plays really are not for children,' she said. 'Playhouses are rough and vulgar and those who go there are mostly untrustworthy rogues. I shall send Jack, the tall boatman from our steps, to fetch you home sharp at nine.'

Later that evening Christopher and Catherine stood at the side of the stage, watching. The play was in full swing, though a lot of it was beyond the understanding of the children. However the audience seemed to be enjoying it in a rough, noisy way.

'At least nobody's thrown anything yet,' said one of two fine ladies in rich costume, standing by the twins and waiting to go on to do their part.

Christopher nudged Catherine. The younger lady was adjusting her long wig, and when she saw the children watching she grinned and said in quite a deep voice, 'Now then, big eyes, my name's Walter. How do you like my dress?'

'Walter?' gasped Christopher in amazement. 'But if you're a man why are you dressed like a lady?'

Walter looked pleased. 'Do I really look like a woman? I'm supposed to be a princess of France. But didn't you know that girls don't go on the stage — all the female parts are taken by boys. My serving girl here is James.'

At that very moment the boy called James put his hand up to his head, turned as white as a sheet and looked as if he were going to be sick. Then with a little groan he fainted in a heap at their feet.

Pandemonium broke out! Everybody rushed about, James's face was fanned with a kerchief, and smouldering straw was thrust in his face to revive him. Slowly he opened his eyes, looked round and said, 'I feel sick. I ate too many oysters for supper. I shan't be able to go on tonight!' And he gave another groan and staggered away.

There was a moment's silence. Then Walter and the red-bearded actor suddenly caught Christopher by the arm. 'Here, lad,' said Walter. 'Here's your big chance. Put James's dress on and go on in his place.'

'Nay, I dare not,' said Christopher. But Catherine snatched the dress and said, 'I will see he wears it.'

Once she got Christopher behind the stage Catherine said, 'Now, get this on! We cannot let our new friends down.'

'No. I will not,' said Christopher. 'I will never wear a girl's dress!'

'Then I will,' said his sister, and in a second she had slipped the gaudy dress over the top of her own. She flicked her long fair hair until it hung straight like her brother's and slipped back to the waiting actors.

'I've changed my mind,' she said, pretending to be Christoper. 'I will do it. Tell me what to do.'

The red-bearded actor thrust a script into her hand and gave her a push on to the stage. 'Good luck, lad,' he said.

Catherine remembered very little of that strange night. She remembered the creaking floorboards of the stage and the upturned faces of the audience. She remembered the smell of unwashed bodies and the heat of the crowded theatre. The script was written in a spidery hand and she had difficulty in reading it, but nobody seemed to notice as they were all looking at Walter who was speaking in a mincing voice with a French accent.

After a minute or two Catherine was aware that her brother and Jack the boatman were standing at the back of the theatre, looking horrified. But then an event on the stage put an end to things as far as she was concerned.

She had noticed for some time a dandy of a young man from the audience sitting on a stool at the side of the stage. He kept getting in the way of the actors, but he didn't seem to care. People in the crowd below him shouted at him to get off the stage but he just sat there calmly as if he owned the place. Soon one of his friends joined him and they began to talk and laugh loudly, which didn't please the actors at all.

Finally a hand reached up from the audience, grabbed the leg of the young dandy's stool and tugged. With a horrified screech the man fell backwards off the stage. His friend stood up and started to draw his sword. Instantly the air was full of flying apple cores and the whole audience broke into an uproar. The actors fled the stage, pulling Catherine off with them.

'Well,' said Red-beard. 'What a performance! How did you like your first experience of acting, young Christopher?' He looked closely for the first time at the

youngster in the dress. 'It is Christopher, isn't it?' he said doubtfully. 'Surely it isn't . . .?'

But at that moment Aunt Mary and Christopher himself appeared and Catherine was grabbed and rushed out of the theatre at top speed. Later a servant was sent back with the costume, and that was the last the Globe Theatre heard of its newest actor.

'Did you have a good time in London?' asked Mr. Jackson when they finally arrived safely home to Boston. The twins had already found out that their mother had fully recovered and there had been a joyful reunion.

'Yes, thank you, father,' said Catherine.

'But I learned one very strange fact.'

'Oh, and what is that?'

'Why, that girls don't go on the stage!'

The standard and the ring

A small group of horse riders jogged quietly along a
country lane towards the city of York. Their leader,
Colonel Charles Norton, rode in front on his huge grey
war-horse, its leather harness gleaming dully in the
morning sunshine.

By his side rode his daughter Hannah on a brown
pony, laughing and chattering as they went along.
Behind them, two by two, came a small troop of
dragoons, well-armed and stern-faced.

'Will you get to see the King, father?' asked Hannah. She looked proudly at her father's rich clothes, lace cuffs, and sweeping feather.

'Yes, Hannah,' he said. 'When the army meets near Oxford there will be many old friends for me to greet. Your Uncle Richard will be there, for sure, and your cousins Edward and Edgar. And my old friend and comrade Edward Verney will be there with his sons. I hear that he is to carry the King's standard into battle. All the good Royalist families will be riding like us to rally round our King, God bless him.'

'Why can't I come as far as Oxford with you?' said Hannah, pouting a little. 'I should very much like to see my cousins again.'

'Why, child,' laughed her father, 'your cousins are both grown men now, ready to fight for their King against the Parliamentary troops. They will not want to be bothered with little girls at a time like this!'

Hannah would have argued, but just at that moment they came in sight of a roadside blacksmith's cottage. The forge was roaring and there was the ringing sound of hammer on hot iron.

'Pardon, sir,' called out one of the dragoons. 'Perhaps it would be wise to get a few loose shoes tightened. We have a long ride ahead.'

Colonel Norton reined in and spoke with the men. Then he and Hannah and two soldiers rode on while the rest of the troop dismounted and stayed behind. Arrangements were made for them all to meet again in York.

The bell of the clock on York Minster was chiming midday as the little party trotted through Bootham Bar and reined in under the walls of York Castle. Colonel Norton dismounted, stretched his legs and lifted Hannah down from her pony.

'Now, my dear,' he said, a little gruffly but kissing her fondly. 'Be a good girl while I am away. It will not be long before we have thrashed the enemy, and then I shall be home again. Now, I have a friend to see in the city here. Tom and Allan will see you safe home again. Up you get, and good-bye.'

Hannah put her foot into the stirrup, but just as she did so another bunch of horsemen clattered round a corner and drew up in a cloud of dust not far away. At first she thought that they were the dragoons back from the shoesmith, but then she saw that these men were dressed in dark clothes and steel armour. Their leader was a burly, dark man with a pale face and a drooping moustache. Hannah recognized him as a landowner whose grounds came close to those of her father. She heard Colonel Norton draw in a sharp breath and Tom and Allan got off their horses again and stood close.

'Atkisson,' said Tom. 'It's Atkisson, sir, him as joined the Parliament army!'

'I know him well enough,' said the Colonel. 'Haste you, Tom, away with the child now. Allan, stay with me.' He bent down and hoisted Hannah into her saddle, giving her no time to argue. But before they could ride away Atkisson shouted something in a mocking voice and his companions guffawed. The Colonel flushed with anger.

'Have you no manners, Atkisson?' he called. 'You can see that I have my daughter here.'

Atkisson looked up. 'It would have been better for her if she had been the daughter of a cowman rather than the daughter of the lackey of a foolish king!'

'Traitor!' roared the Colonel. 'Villain!' He strode over to Atkisson and his men. Hannah saw Atkisson pull something from his belt, then there was a bright flash and a loud explosion. She saw her father stagger back, hand up to his face. She screamed and her pony reared and whinnied with fright.

However, the Colonel was not badly hurt. He recovered and plunged forward again. He caught Atkisson by his broad leather belt, and with one heave fetched him headlong from the saddle so that he fell sprawling and cursing on the dusty cobblestones.

From then on all was noise and confusion. Atkisson's soldiers came at Hannah's father with the butt ends of their muskets and she saw him fall senseless into the ditch at the side of the road.

One of the men dismounted and raised his musket again but Tom was there and hit him at the back of the knees with the flat of his sword. The man fell screaming.

Allan now swung his cutlass at Atkisson himself who was struggling up from the cobbles. Atkisson dodged, but Allan caught him a tremendous kick on the thigh. Hannah heard a sharp sound like a stick snapping and Atkisson stumbled again to the floor.

The skirmish was over. Atkisson's men carried him away, and from the way he dragged his leg it appeared as if it were broken.

Allan and Tom carefully lifted Colonel Norton from the ditch and helped him into a nearby inn, where he regained consciousness quite quickly. Hannah covered the burn on his forehead caused by the blast of the pistol, and she put his injured right arm into a rough sling. He winced as she touched it.

'I fear your arm may be broken, father,' she said. The Colonel nodded and sighed.

'Then the war is over for me,' he said. 'Instead of fighting for the king at a glorious battle, I end up brawling with a neighbour in a town street. That man Atkisson was eating at my table last Christmas, Hannah, and laughing with my family in my house. What sort of country are we living in where two neighbours break each other's bones?'

The rest of the dragoons had by now arrived from the shoesmith. After a long conversation with them, Colonel Norton again spoke to Hannah.

'Hannah, I want you to do something very brave for me. I want you to change from your dress into boy's clothes and to ride to Oxford with the men. You will be quite safe dressed as a boy and in the care of Tom and Allan.'

Hannah gasped with surprise, but before she could say anything her father went on: 'Once you get to Oxford, find your Uncle Richard. Tell him what has happened to me and deliver him this very important letter for the King's own hands. It names all the loyal folk round York, and says who will support him.'

Hannah took the folded paper. 'But, father,' she said. 'Not long ago you said that I should never go near the battle, and yet now you are sending me off to war! What a change!'

'Not to war, child, to Oxford only! Come closer and listen.' He drew her head down and whispered in her ear. 'The letter is not really important. But these dragoons are not all that keen to fight. Now that I am not able to lead them they may well desert. But they are loyal to the family and they will take you to Oxford where your Uncle Richard will see that they join the King's army and fight for him. The King needs every able-bodied man if he is to keep his crown, and it is up to you to see that these dragoons are there when needed!'

Hannah did not like leaving her father. But he called for the lady of the inn and before too long Hannah was dressed in boy's shirt and breeches. She put her own leather tunic over her head and slipped into her riding boots. With her long hair fastened back she looked every inch a boy and she was quite pleased with her appearance.

Minutes later they were all in their saddles and cantering out of York on the start of the long journey to Oxford.

It took four days of hard riding, stopping at night at friendly houses. It all seemed like a dream but at last they were within sight of the city of Oxford with its spires and towers and grey stone college walls. The city teemed with Royalist troops and the streets were crowded and dirty. The noise was deafening and everywhere there seemed to be the smell of food cooking for the thousands of men filling the town.

Hannah made enquiries for her Uncle and was directed to a small inn near All Saints. Sir Richard did not recognize her in her boy's clothes, but when he did so he threw his arms round her and gave her a great hug. He was distressed to hear of his brother's condition, but scanned the letter he had sent and then hurried away with it to the King. Hannah was left with her cousins Edgar and Edward.

Edward slapped her on her back and teased his small cousin, whom he had last seen as a very young girl. 'Will you come to the war, then, little man?' he said with a grin. Hannah frowned. 'Yes, if you will take me,' she said stoutly.

The young men both roared with laughter and called her a little fighting cock. But Hannah was serious and before too long, a little to their surprise, the brothers found themselves agreeing to hide Hannah in their baggage train so that she could watch the troops drawing up round the King's standard.

'That far and no further,' Edgar said. 'If and when the battle begins, you go back to the baggage women and ride home. Do you promise?'

'I promise,' said Hannah, wild with excitement. But promises are too easily broken, and as soon as the King's army came within sight of the Parliament army at Edgehill, the brothers forgot their young cousin in the dash and confusion.

When she came to tell her story later Hannah remembered very little about the battle. She could not see much for the smoke. It seemed like a wild confusion of noise and rushing about. Nobody seemed to know what to do or where to go, and there were little skirmishes going on all over the place.

Once she saw a glorious charge of Royalist cavalry driving all before them. At another time she watched hedgehogs of pikemen struggling with each other some way away. But for the most part she saw no further than a few paces, and only knew what was going on very close to her.

At first she was being looked after by Jason, the servant of her father's old friend, Sir Edward Verney. He was a gruff old countryman and was distressed to see her caught up in the battle.

Then, after the first great Royalist cavalry charge they found themselves attacked by a group of Parliamentary soldiers. Poor Jason was killed instantly with one slash of a cutlass and Hannah fell to the ground at his side, unhurt but very frightened.

She heard Sir Edward cry out with anger as he saw
his servant die, and saw the royal standard which he was
carrying flutter in the air. Two of the Parliamentary
soldiers fell under his sword, and then he too fell and the
standard was trampled in the mud.

Hannah screamed and started to crawl towards the
flag through the clods of turf and the mud and litter of
the battle. Her own hands and face were blood-stained
and scratched, and tears ran down her cheeks. But just as
she reached out for the fallen standard it was snatched up
by a Parliamentary soldier who brandished it over his
head in triumph.

'Look, comrades,' he yelled. 'I have the standard of the traitor Charles. The day is ours!'

Hannah screamed again, this time with anger as well as fear, and then dimly through her tears she saw a cavalry officer whom she recognized galloping towards her. He seemed to be cut off from the Royalist troops and was spurring his horse to rejoin them.

'Captain Smith! Captain Smith!' yelled Hannah. 'They are taking away the standard! Stop them!'

The Parliamentary soldier heard her cry and turned. He saw a mud-stained small boy in front of him and instead of running him through with his raised sword he caught him a smack with the back of his hand. But as Hannah fell she saw Captain Smith grab the standard and gallop away shouting.

For the next hour Hannah lay, half-senseless from the soldier's blow, among the bodies of the dead and wounded. The noise of battle came and went, but she dared not move too much in case enemy soldiers took her captive. She did manage to reach Sir Edward but he was dead also, and Hannah wept bitterly.

As she lay there she saw that the knight's left hand was slightly open and that a gold ring gleamed on his finger. Turning over the palm she saw that the ring had a beautiful miniature portrait of the King on it, and rather than leave it for some scavenger to steal she slipped it off and pushed it on to her thumb.

Gradually the roar of battle died down, and Hannah was able to crawl away, then to stand with aching limbs, and finally to hobble off in the direction of Oxford. She had not gone too far when she found a riderless horse, mounted it, and completed her journey quickly and in comfort.

When she got to the city she found that all was in confusion. Troops were bringing in dead and wounded from the battlefield and others were packing their baggage carts to move hastily away. Rumour said that the King had fled the field of battle, but others said that he was in pursuit of fleeing Parliamentary troops. Nobody seemed to know what to do, but many of the King's followers were taking their men and going home.

Hannah searched the streets for a friendly face, but everyone seemed to be too busy to take any notice of a dirty-faced boy on a large horse.

Then at last she found Tom and Allan, both weary from the fight. Allan had a bandage round his head after a cut from a sword, but Tom had escaped scot-free. They were overjoyed to see their young mistress, for they had been fearing that she was lost and that they would have a hard job explaining to Colonel Norton what had happened to her. They heard her story with amazement and shook their heads when they heard how close she had been to death.

'We must get away from this city,' said Tom. 'Some say the enemy troops will be here within the hour!'

The way home was long and dangerous. They dodged various groups of skirmishing troops, and had to avoid hostile towns and villages. News of the great battle of Edgehill was spreading fast and soldiers were not welcome anywhere.

It was with a great deal of relief that they finally cantered through the iron gates of Hannah's home and heard them clang shut behind them.

Colonel Norton made his daughter tell him her story over and over again. He was saddened by the news she gave of the death of his old friend Sir Edward Verney, and he was worried when Hannah told him that she had no news of the fate of her cousins or uncle. They would have to wait many days to learn what had happened to them.

'But this is a marvellous ring,' he said when Hannah prised it off her thumb and showed it to him. 'We must see that Sir Edward's son gets it as soon as possible, together with your news about the brave way his father

died.' He rubbed at the miniature portrait of the King and wiped a speck of mud away from it. When he looked up again his eyes were filled with tears.

'Sir Edward is dead,' he said, 'and I fear for the life of the man in this portrait. This war will last a long time now, and the country will not recover for years. My fighting days are over, since my arm will never be strong enough to wield a sword again. Indeed my fighting days hardly started!'

He looked tenderly at his daughter. 'But you, Hannah, took the honour of the Norton family into battle, and carried yourself well. I am truly proud of my daughter.'

Hannah smiled back at him, but in her heart she was vowing that she would never again go anywhere near a battle, nor would she dress in boy's clothes. Whether King or Parliament finally won was unimportant to her. What mattered was that she and her family were all safe in their Yorkshire home.

Pictures on the wall

Reign of William and Mary

It was spring 1700 and the woods were bursting with life.
Jane Earle ran happily along a grassy path, stopping
now and again to pick up fallen fir cones and examine
them for squirrel bites.

Once she knelt to smell a pale dog-violet sheltering
under the broad hairy leaves of a young foxglove. As she

stooped there the smell of woodsmoke came drifting
through the trees and Jane smiled. Quickly she got to her
feet again and ran on round a bend in the path.

Before long Jane came to a clearing in the wood. A
rough shelter of brushwood leaned against a grassy bank
at one side. There were piles of slender sticks nearby, and
here and there blackened patches on the ground showed
where large fires had burned.

Three or four dome-shaped mounds were dotted about
the clearing, each one giving out a curling wisp of grey
smoke. These were the charcoal heaps built by Jane's
father, Walter, and Walter himself was there, sitting with
his back to a stump of wood, yawning.

'Hello, father,' Jane called cheerfully.

Walter Earle got up and stretched his arms. He was
tired. Since the first spring day he had been working long
hours, cutting wood, heaping branches and soil, burning
and raking, sifting and carting. At nights he had
snatched a little sleep under the rough shelter, but it was
tiring work. He was pleased to see his daughter and
thought immediately how tall she was getting.

'Is all well?' he asked as they kissed in greeting. It
was several days since he had been home to see the
family.

'Mother is well, and so are the little ones,' said Jane
with a smile. 'But I have some news, father.'

'News? News of what?'

'News of me! I have a job. I am to go into service at
Ashtead Park this very day. I have come to fetch you
home so that we can say farewell properly.'

Walter's face fell. He knew, of course, that for some time now Jane had talked of taking a job as a servant at one of the large houses nearby. Her success would mean one less mouth for him to feed, but the thought of not seeing his eldest child again except on her two days' holiday each year upset him and made him sad.

'Well then,' he said, 'Living in a fine house you will soon forget me.' He hugged his daughter with affection. Jane grinned and pushed him away, brushing crumbs of leaf-mould from her dress.

'How could I forget you? The dirt you've just put on me will take at least a year to wash off,' she laughed. They walked slowly back to the cottage, joking together.

Jane's mother met them at the door of their home. She had cooked a meal of new bread and pea-soup and they ate in the big room, the three of them sitting on rough stools near the open doorway while the younger children played outside.

Then, all too soon, the meal was over and Jane had to set off to her first job. Indeed it was the first time she had been away from home. Walter walked with her to the edge of the woods and watched her as she stepped lightly down the rutted track that led to the village. There it had been arranged that she would get a lift on Phil the Carrier's cart to Ashtead Park.

Jane was an easy-going girl and she quickly settled down in her new life. She shared a large attic room at the back of the house, sleeping there with three other servant girls of about the same age.

She was given a new black dress and a cap and apron, and had to get used to wearing boots instead of going barefoot. For a time she felt stifled in the thick new clothes and thought often of the freedom of her past life in the woods.

However she was kept too busy to do much thinking. Her master, Sir Robert Howard, liked entertaining and Ashtead Park was usually full of visitors staying with Sir Robert and his large family.

The four girls had to clean out the grates and light the fires, sweep and dust the vast rooms, and wash and care for the displays of china ware. Food had to be fetched and carried from the home farm and from the village nearby. The padded door on the double-walled ice-house in the grounds had to be forced open, and blocks of dripping ice dragged back to the kitchens. Jane found that there was always somebody nearby to tell her what to do and somebody else to shout at her for not doing it fast enough!

But, for all that, there were many times when she enjoyed her life. She liked it best in the late evening when all four of the girls, snuggled underneath the thick bedclothes in the draughty attic, laughed and giggled and chattered. They would frighten themselves by telling each other ghost stories and shiver as the pale candle flame sent long shadows sprawling across the room.

Jane also enjoyed peeping out of the bedroom windows and looking down on the gravelled drive as the carriages arrived with new visitors. She liked to see the grand clothes and sparkling jewels of the guests, and would marvel at their strange speech and even stranger manners. She would watch with round eyes as they ate and drank at the huge polished table in the dining room and often thought how sad it was to see so much food cooked and then not eaten.

One day, when she had been there about six months, there came great news. The house was to be visited by Princess Anne, daughter to the King and heiress to the throne of England! Jane and her friends got very excited at the thought of seeing a real princess.

'What is she like?' she asked her friend Judith, as they struggled into clean white aprons. Judith frowned. She was having some difficulty settling the white lace cap on her thick red hair. With a mouth full of pins she mumbled, 'Why she's old enough to be your mother, stoops like a carrion crow, has pock-marked skin and drinks herself unconscious every night!'

Jane was astonished, but at the same time she knew that Judith often told tall stories so she decided to wait and see for herself. She had hoped to see a beautiful princess.

'Drinks, did you say?' said Jane. 'What is it that she drinks?'

Judith laughed. 'Cold tea, they call it, 'cause she will have it served in a teapot, but folks don't call her "Brandy Nan" for nothing!'

At that moment they heard a voice calling them to help set the big table for dinner. First of all they took off the old cloth which was badly stained with sauces and gravies and was extremely dirty. Judith wrinkled her nose. 'Here,' she said, crumpling it into Jane's arms, 'take this horrible thing away. I'm sure that it's been on the table since Christmas!'

Jane stood with the dirty linen in her arms. 'What shall I do with it?' she asked.

Judith sighed. 'Well we shall have to wash it eventually, but for the moment put it outside in the outhouse. Tomorrow we must start all the soaking and beating and rubbing in of lye. We shall be a month of Sundays before that's white again!'

When Jane got back to the dining room she saw that a new white cloth had been spread on the table, but even this one had a few dull stains that washing and boiling had failed to get out.

'Here, cover that nasty stain in the middle with this crock,' said Judith. 'It's the pot they throw their bones in when they've finished chewing at them. I daresay they miss the pot as often as they hit it, especially when the wine has been going round. That accounts for every cloth having a great grease-spot in that place.'

They set out scrubbed wooden trenchers and some fine gold plate at the place where the Princess would be sitting. A silver goblet was by each place. Then forks were produced, rubbed with sand and salt to clean them, and laid on the table. Jane picked one up and looked at it curiously.

'What's this?' she asked.

'It's called a fork,' replied Judith. 'It's for spearing pieces of food with. Folks say that it's cleaner and easier than just using a knife and fingers, but I've never tried it. I can't imagine why anyone would want to fiddle with a thing like that.'

Jane thought of her mother and father and how astonished they would be when she told them of the split spoons rich folk used to eat their food.

Later that evening Jane and Judith had to help carry in the food and serve it, so they had a good look at Princess Anne. She wasn't quite as bad as Judith had said, but she was very plain, no longer young, and had a face that never seemed to smile. She ate and drank a lot but said very little.

Towards the end of the meal Jane felt a nudge in her ribs and turned to see Judith, with a face as white as a sheet, beckoning her behind a screen.

'What's the matter?' she said.

Judith was trembling. 'Jane, there's wickedness going on here, wickedness and witchcraft, you mark my words.'

The mention of witchcraft made Jane cover her face with her hands in horror. 'What do you mean?' she asked. But Judith would say only a little more: 'The men have put big black curtains up in the withdrawing room, and the place is as dark and creepy as the graveyard. And in one corner they've set up a big black box on legs. But that's not the worst — out of one side of that black box there's a huge eye, like a bull's-eye, peering out at us!'

The girls went back to the table. By this time Princess Anne had chewed and spluttered her way through a large bowl of rabbit and chicken joints, followed by slices from a boiled leg of mutton. Some of the guests had dug into three fat baked carp while others had enjoyed roast pigeons and lamb chops. Ten lobsters were then brought in and quickly torn to pieces and eaten, as was a huge lamprey pie, three round fruit tarts, and a platter of salted anchovies.

Sir Robert belched comfortably and lifted his goblet to the Princess. 'We should have had oysters, your Highness,' he said, 'but it's been a bad season and they're asking two shillings a hundred for them. That's a bit much even for me.' The Princess's face broke into a faint uninterested smile and she took a large gulp of wine.

Now the bowls and trenchers were cleared away and great silver stands were placed on the table, filled with piles of oranges, almonds, raisins, comfits, and marzipan confections. More bottles were fetched up from the cellar and the noise round the table began to get louder.

Jane had not forgotten what Judith had said and strained her ears to try to catch what the guests were talking about. One old lady, crushing ice into an orange said, 'This reminds me of how old Francis died.'

'Francis?' said her neighbour, spitting out a piece of lobster shell which had been stuck in his tooth.

'Francis Bacon, Lord Verulam! Don't you remember how he thought he could preserve food by packing it in ice? Had a shocking cold one winter. Stopped his coach on the way home and got down in the cold night air to stuff chickens with snow to prove his point. Caught his death he did. The chickens lasted longer than he did, eh? Heh, heh!'

She chuckled her way through her orange while her neighbour fiddled with his tongue round his cracked and blackened teeth for another piece of lobster shell.

Suddenly Sir Robert rose to his feet. 'Your Royal Highness,' he said, 'and friends. Finish off your drinks for I have a fine piece of devilment for your entertainment. Our friend here, Hans, has brought his magic box to show us!'

There was a happy buzz of excitement, but Jane felt weak at the knees. 'Devilment', Sir Robert had said. And 'magic'.

The guests trooped out into the withdrawing room where tall candles had been lit. The great sash windows were firmly shuttered and heavy curtains had been drawn across to cut out any stray moonbeams. From the wall above the empty fireplace the great painted portrait of Sir Robert's father had been removed, leaving a large square white patch on the plaster.

Jane and Judith stood in the shadows at the back of the room, hardly daring to breathe. Then Sir Robert stood up. 'Now, Hans,' he said, 'Where's your magic box, then? Are you ready?'

Hans, a portly old man with a foreign-sounding voice, bowed and went nervously to the back of the room where the black box stood on its legs. A fat, round glass window, which Judith had called an eye, stuck out at the front of the box. Hans lifted up a hinged wooden door at the back and reached inside with a lighted candle. Smoke came drifting out of a stubby metal chimney on top and then a beam of light shone out of the eye making a bright white patch of light on the wall. Jane shivered.

'It's something like my father's storm lantern,' she whispered, 'but what a bright light he's getting out of it!'

'That must be for the Devil to dance in,' said Judith with chattering teeth. 'Oh Lord preserve us!'

Hans now produced several long strips of glass and pushed the end of one into the side of the box. Instantly a blurred picture appeared on the wall. Jane and several ladies in the audience screamed faintly, but Sir Robert called out, 'It's all right! It's all right! Snuff out the candles so that we can see better!'

With the room in darkness the picture could be seen clearly. It was of a foreign-looking man with a heavy beard.

'It's the Devil!' shivered Judith. Her hand in Jane's was icy.

'This is a picture of Herr Kircher, who in 1646 wrote a description of the working of the magic lantern,' announced Hans in a loud voice. Several people clapped. The picture vanished and its place was taken by a detailed painting of a huge building.

'Saint Paul's Cathedral, in London,' said Hans. The next picture was of the Palace at Westminster and there followed several more of public buildings. Then came one of a fat milk-cow which caused a lot of laughter. Even the Princess who was sipping something from a tea cup, let a smile appear on her face.

'That's my prize cow,' said Sir Robert. 'Hans had these slides painted specially for me! Now for some real magic, for you will see him make the cow move!'

Hans deftly moved the slide strip along so that more pictures were seen in quick succession. As each slide was a picture of the same cow in a slightly different position it could have been thought that a real cow was walking across the wall! Loud applause greeted the end of the sequence.

'Bravo!' said the Princess with a loud hiccough. 'We should like to see that again!' And so she did.

'Finally,' said Hans, 'I shall make real moving pictures. Watch, please.'

On the screen came a brightly painted picture of a windmill. Hans jerked a small brass knob at the side of the machine and as he did so the arms of the windmill seemed to rotate.

Gasps of astonishment rose from the audience and this piece of magic proved to be too much for the terrified Judith. She burst into tears and flew out of the room, followed by Jane, and they did not stop until they were safe upstairs in their own room with their heads buried under the bedclothes.

Next morning when the Princess had gone, Sir Robert sent for the two girls, and insisted that Hans showed them the inside of his black box. 'See,' he said, 'It is not witchcraft but just a very special trick.'

Jane and Judith were still doubtful. 'If you say so, sir,' said Jane with a curtsey, 'but it did seem to me that those windmill arms were moving!'

Sir Robert laughed and fumbled in a fob pocket. 'Here,' he said. 'Here's a new shilling for each of you. Tomorrow is quarter-day so you can collect your half-year's wages and take the day off to go home. That should rid your heads of witchcraft.'

And so, next day, clutching her tapestry purse in which were her wages of five shillings for half a year and the shilling Sir Robert had given her, Jane made her way home again. She smiled as she thought of how she would tell her younger brothers and sisters of the magic lantern, and carefully rehearsed her final speech, when she would amaze them by saying, 'And there, on the wall, as big as the giant Blunderbore, was a huge windmill, waving its sails around for all the world as if it were really in the room with us!'

'Charge!' *Victorian*

These are extracts from the diary of Captain Charles
Quincy Tanglynge-Smythe, late of the Dragoon Guards,
concerning his brave deeds in the Crimean War.

July 1854. On board HMS 'Renown' off the
Dardanelles Strait. It's been a very bad day, as the
regiment is cooped up on this stinking ship like cattle.
There is nowhere for a gentleman to stroll, and in any
case the weather is stiflingly hot. Even worse, I am
having to share a sleeping cabin with three other officers.

One of these is Bertie Lawrence, a man I dislike for
his sneering tongue. Only this morning, for example, I
happened to say that I was looking forward to stretching
my legs ashore.

'Stretching your legs!' sneered Lawrence, twirling his thick cavalry moustache. You'll need to do more than that to be of any use. You've never been in action have you?'

I said that I had not, though I had attended several exercises on the cliffs at Brighton. That seemed to amuse him.

'That's not action! I thought your boots looked clean! Wait until you've done what I've had to do — lie on snow-covered hill-tops with your belly rumbling from hunger and Russian bullets whistling round your head. You won't bother about your boots then!'

Lawrence is no gentleman. I shall always bother about my boots. A man who lets his boots get muddy cannot be a good soldier, and I told him so, but he just laughed and said, 'You wait and see!'

September 1854. Near Sebastopol on the Crimean Peninsula. A relief to get off the ship. We are part of a mixed British, French, and Turkish army. The French are all right, except that they do seem to dash around all the time, shouting and waving their arms about. I was sitting having my breakfast today, when one of the fellows came rushing up.

I said to him, 'I say, old chap, why don't you sit down and have a rest for a bit? You make me feel tired with all that rushing around.'

But he just seemed to fly into a temper and jabbered away in French, turning quite nasty when I just sat there on my camp-stool.

Apparently, as I found out later, his men had come under sharp fire from Russian troops and he had wanted me to take my men to help him. Well how was I to know? He ought to have learned English when he knew he was going to deal with British officers.

October 1854. A terrible mix-up happened today. I still cannot fathom out what really went wrong or whose fault it all was, but it resulted in an awful loss of life among our fellows.

Just along the line from us were the Light Brigade. Nice mounts they had, and their chaps knew all about cleaning horse-brasses, I can tell you. Very smart and impressive they were when they jingled past.

I got quite friendly with one of their officers, a chap called Joss Stokes who turned out to be second cousin to old Roland Stokes who was at school with me.

Anyway, when I saw Joss yesterday he reckoned that the Russians had been shooting off their field guns against British cavalry riding along the ridge close by.

'Dashed unsporting of them,' he said. 'Just like shooting sitting ducks. Killed half-a-dozen of our finest nags, and quite a few of our men were hurt too. Why can't they use swords, like us?' I noticed that he had a lovely polish on the hilt of his sabre.

Anyway, I now hear that the following day there was a real muddle at Headquarters, and the Light Brigade were just told to charge down the valley at the enemy guns! I suppose somebody gave the wrong order, or somebody didn't hear it properly. But whatever the reason, an order is an order, and so off went the whole Brigade, first at a trot, then at a canter, and finally charging full-tilt with their sabres drawn, straight at the Russian guns.

I couldn't see what went on from where I was, but there was a great deal of smoke and I could hear the guns blazing away like mad. That awful cad, Lawrence, was standing near me, and he was as white as a sheet.

'Madmen!' he kept saying. 'Madmen! They'll all be slaughtered and blown to bits!'

Of course, he didn't appreciate how marvellous they looked as they rode off down the valley. But it's true that most of them were killed or wounded. It's a terrible loss.

They say the Light Brigade is finished. I hope Joss is all right. As he said, if only the Russians had been gentlemen and fought with swords, things might have been different.

March 1855. The war drags on, but I have had a most unfortunate accident with very unpleasant results, so that I am now writing this in a hospital bed near Sebastopol.

What happened was this. Bertie Lawrence and I were detailed by the Colonel to take out a skirmishing party in order to find out the strength of the Russian troops to the north of the town. We took ten good men. Things started off badly, however, because my new boots had just arrived from England and they were a bit tight round the calves. Lawrence had his usual sneer at me.

'You're walking like a paralysed duck, Charles,' he said, in front of the men too. I do wish he would not use my Christian name.

'Captain Tanglynge-Smythe to you,' I retorted but he pretended not to hear.

'Come on, man,' he said, 'or the war will be over before we get there.'

Well, to cut a long story short, we cantered over to a small wood and dismounted. Lawrence led the way through the trees until we could see the Russian lines down below. Then he sent men out to scout.

'Count the number of field guns,' he said, 'and try to estimate the number of cavalrymen and foot-soldiers as well. Charles, the best thing you can do is to stay here and take the reports as they come in. You should be able to manage that.'

So I stayed in the wood and after a while found myself completely alone. Suddenly out of the trees burst a huge and ferocious Russian soldier, all beard and whiskers, swinging a bloodstained cutlass and yelling like a madman.

I reached for my sabre, but it somehow got tangled up with my new spurs. Fortunately, just as the monster took a swing at me, I tripped over my boots and fell flat on my face in a puddle of mud. Then I heard a grunt and something warm and heavy landed on top of me. At the same time something sharp dug into my leg and I lost consciousness.

When I woke up Lawrence was standing over me, grinning like an idiot and wiping the blade of his sabre. The Russian was flat on his back and dead.

'Well, Charles,' said Lawrence, 'it was a good job I came along when I did. There you were flat on your face while this chap was about to skewer you like a fly to the ground!'

'So what happened?' I asked.

'Oh, I put paid to him just in time. It was bad luck that he dropped his sword as he fell and it gave you a nasty gash in the leg. It looks like hospital for you, my lad, since you've been wounded in action!'

He is an awful sort, and I shall not be sorry if I never see him again, even if he did save my life.

So here I am in bed in hospital. It is a fairly dreadful place. There's a dragon of a person called Miss Nightingale who seems to be in charge of the place, and who keeps giving orders to everybody in a no-nonsense sort of voice. The ordinary soldiers seem to love her, though. She spoils them, of course, coming round during the long nights with a little yellow lantern and talking with them. She sees that they have clean blankets — first time in their lives for some of these fellows, I'll be bound — and gives them much the same care as she gives to the officers. That can't be right.

She's too fond of telling folk what to do for my liking, and only the other day told me to clean my own boots when I asked one of the nurses to do it for me. Reminds me of that awful chap Lawrence. A woman's place is in the home, and I told her so!

Anyway I'm getting better from my wound and I find that I've been recommended for a medal for bravery in action. Peace is in the air, too, so I suppose I shall soon be sailing back to England, which will be a good thing.

One of the first things I shall have to do is to buy some new clothes. I find that that scoundrel Lawrence actually slit my new boot with a knife to get my wounded leg out of it! Slit it from top to bottom and never mind the expense! The latest news about him is that he's being promoted to Colonel because of outstanding service. I can't understand it myself. A man who didn't even keep his boots clean. The British Army just doesn't have high enough standards any more.

Doctor Baird's magic box

Early 20th century

Mrs Tickle was a charlady. Every morning at seven o'clock sharp she reported for work at a large stone building in the centre of London and spent the next two hours scrubbing the rooms and corridors.

Her husband, Mr Tickle, worked down at the docks in the East End. His job was hard and called for strong men who could work all day heaving sacks and heavy boxes from ship to shore. But Mrs Tickle thought very little of what her husband did, and wished he had a different job.

'George,' she would say as she clattered about in the tiny back-kitchen of their little home. 'What have you been doing today?'

'Beef, today,' said Mr Tickle contentedly from where he sat in their one armchair reading the evening paper borrowed from next door. 'Load of salt beef from South America. Tons of it, we had to shift, tons.'

Mrs Tickle snorted over the sink. She was a rather stout lady with red hair and freckles.

'That's not difficult,' she said. 'I bet you could train monkeys to do that.' She had once been to London Zoo on her birthday and had been much taken with the chimpanzees' tea party.

Mr Tickle did not answer. He went on reading about the Arsenal football team.

Mrs Tickle went on about George's job. 'Monkeys, that's what you are down there in the docks. Just trained monkeys. What you need is a modern sort of job, one that uses your brains.'

'I've got no brains,' said Mr Tickle, 'only brawn. And anyway I like the job. It's interesting, seeing ships come in from all over the world. Last week it was chests of tea from Ceylon. The week before great loads of frozen sheep came in from New Zealand and timber from Sweden. It's a very interesting job and it's hard work, whatever you say.'

But Mrs Tickle still hadn't finished. 'The gentlemen who work at my place,' she said, meaning the large building she helped to clean, 'have to use brain, not brawn. Always got clean hands, they have. And with their money their wives don't have to go out charring, I can tell you.'

George looked at his large, red hands with their split nails and rough skin. He grunted and folded up the paper. 'I can see it's going to be one of those nights,' he said with a sigh. 'So while you stay here and nag, I'm off to the pub to see the other monkeys.'

Nellie Tickle went to work next morning on her usual early bus. The ride cost her twopence return which made a shilling a week out of the pound she earned. But it was a lot quicker and easier than walking, and cheaper than the underground trains.

She looked out of the window of the big red bus at the early morning streets, thinking about what she had said to George the night before. Perhaps she had been hard on him. She knew he was good at his work but she really did wish he had a job that used brains. But if he couldn't do that perhaps he could find a job where he was able to look smart. He could have been a policeman like that one down there directing the traffic by the Tower. Or he could have been a floorwalker in one of those posh shops in Regent Street. Perhaps he could have been a commissionaire at a picture palace with a bright blue uniform and gold epaullettes.

Mrs Tickle snorted and said aloud, 'Or a bus conductor!' The conductor smiled at her and pulled the knotted string that rang the bell in the driver's cab. 'Right you are, love,' he said. 'Your stop. The Royal Institution.'

'Here,' said Mrs Tickle to him. 'You don't need any brains in your job do you? My husband could do it easily. How much do you get paid?'

The conductor was used to funny passengers. He just smiled and said, 'Mind the step now.' Then he pulled the bell-cord twice and the bus moved off.

Mrs Tickle said good morning to the hall porter at the Royal Institution where she worked.

'Morning, Nellie,' he replied. 'Do me a favour today. Make a special quick effort with the lecture room. We've got a big do on this morning.' The front hall already smelt of wax polish and the tiles were gleaming wet from being washed over.

Mrs Tickle picked up her bucket and broom from the cleaners' room and took a flowered apron from her carrier bag. 'That will cost you a cup of tea,' she said cheerfully. 'That lecture room's not easy to clean with all those steps and benches. What's on, anyway?'

The porter looked at a programme pinned to the wall of his cubby-hole. 'A demonstration,' he said. 'A Doctor Baird is demonstrating his new invention. There'll be a big crowd.'

'All those clever gentlemen,' sighed Nellie Tickle, 'and I had to settle for a docker.'

Mrs Tickle walked upstairs and pushed open the doors at the back of the lecture theatre. Down below on the platform, a small man with glasses and untidy hair was fiddling about with a lot of wires and boxes.

'Good morning, sir,' said Nellie. 'Can I do this room now?'

The man looked up. 'Eh?' he said. 'Oh. Oh, yes, I suppose so. Are you going to sweep a lot of dust about?'

'No, sir,' said Mrs. Tickle haughtily. 'I'm going to get rid of it for you, not sweep it about, and make the room look all nice for your demonstration.'

'Well, all right then,' said the man, who Nellie guessed must be Dr Baird. 'But be careful of these wires and boxes.'

Mrs Tickle worked quickly and carefully. The bits and pieces on the platform looked strange to her. On the table was a squarish box with a little glass window in the front of it and a knob or two at the back. Wires trailed from it and led into a room off the back of the platform.

For all the world it looked like one of those so-called wireless sets. Mrs Tickle's neighbour, Mrs Ball, had a wireless set and the whole street had been in, in turn, to try on the headphones and wonder at the odd sounds that came when Mr Ball tickled the crystal with what he called a cat's whisker.

'What's that, sir?' asked Nellie as the small man came back into the room. He smiled and did something at the back of the box which made it hum. Then suddenly the glass window glowed with a pale light and lots of little spots flickered across it.

'Just don't touch it,' said Dr Baird. 'I have to go into the back room, so be careful not to dust round the apparatus while I'm away.'

'Apparatus is it?' said Nellie. 'I wonder what an apparatus does. Looks just like my George's rabbit hutch with a window in it.' And she put down her duster and went over to the table. Just then she heard Dr Baird call out from the back room.

'I say, Mrs — er —, can you see that box on the table?'

'My name's Nellie Tickle, and yes, I can see that there box.'

'Tell me exactly what you can see.'

'Its little window is all lit up, like,' said Nellie. 'It's a bit like the screen at the picture palace when the film breaks down.'

'Anything else?'

Mrs Tickle peered at the screen and then gave a little scream. 'Ooh, yes. Now there's a picture come on it, but it's all shaky. I think it's a man.'

'Tell me exactly what you see.'

'Well, it's all sort of misty and there's a lot of spots, and it's crackling. But it's definitely a picture of a man. Here, how do you do that? Where's the thing with the film in?' Mrs Tickle peered suspiciously round the back of the set, as if she half expected to see a little man round there.

'What's the man doing?' came Dr Baird's voice.

'Doing? He's doing nothing of course, since he's just a picture. Here, wait a minute, he's just lifted his arm up. How do you do that?'

'Watch. I'll make him walk towards you.'

The shadowy figure on the screen grew larger until the head and shoulders filled the screen. Nellie peered at the face. Somehow it looked familiar. Then the mouth moved.

'Do you recognize him?' said the voice from the back room. That was funny, thought Nellie. It was just as if the man on the screen had spoken; his mouth had seemed to say the same words. She peered again, and then she gave a little scream.

'Ooh! It's a picture of you!'

The face smiled at her. 'It's not a picture,' said the voice from the back room. 'You're seeing me do things at the same time as I actually do them. A camera in here is sending pictures to that screen in there.'

'I don't understand,' said Nellie. 'How do you make the picture's mouth move as if it was actually speaking?'

'Watch,' said Dr. Baird's voice. 'I'm going to touch my nose.'

A flickering finger came up and touched the nose of the man on the screen.

Mrs Tickle sank into a chair, astonished. 'Here,' she said, 'I can't believe it. Go on, then, if you can do things — close your eyes.'

The face on the screen closed its eyes.

'Touch your ears.'

Two hands came up and pulled the ears of the face on the screen.

'It's just like magic,' said Mrs Tickle.

'I call it "television",' said Dr Baird. The little screen went dark and blank as he came out of the back room. 'And you, Mrs. Tickle, have just seen one of the first demonstrations of a television receiver at work.'

Mrs Tickle could hardly wait to tell her husband what she had seen. She described Dr Baird and his magic box in great detail, and told how she had seen him touching his ears and nose.

George Tickle looked up from his steaming plate of boiled beef and carrots.

'What's clever about that?' he asked. 'If you want to see somebody put his fingers in his ears you can see me! He put his fingers in his ears and stuck his tongue out at the same time. 'In fact, I've seen monkeys do it,' he said with a smile.

Mrs Tickle had to laugh. 'You can make fun of it, George, but I think this television is a wonderful invention. One day everybody may have a television set.'

Her husband put down his knife and fork, wiped his plate clean with a piece of bread and then got up and kissed his wife.

'Well, it sounds pretty unlikely to me, but if you had the choice, would you prefer to sit and watch someone sticking his fingers in his ears all the evening, or come to the pub by the river with me for a glass of stout and a plate of jellied eels.'

Mrs Tickle smiled. 'You're really quite a clever man George,' she said. 'Wait a minute and I'll get my hat and coat.'